Winter Solstice
A Novel

LUCY COSTIGAN

ENLIGHTEN PUBLISHING

PRAISE FOR LUCY COSTIGAN'S BOOKS

Winter Solstice
A Novel

All Rights Reserved © 2014 by Lucy Costigan

The first version of 'Winter Solstice: A Novel' by Lucy Costigan was first published by iUniverse, Inc., NE, USA, in 2003.

Trapped in a Cage © 1990 by Anthony Costigan.

Published 2014
By Enlighten Publishing,
14 Thomas Street,
Wexford,
Ireland
Email: info@enlightenpublishing.com
www.enlightenpublishing.com

ISBN: 978-0-9930188-0-0

Cover Photo: Michael Cullen and Dave Broberg
(www.123rf.com)
Spiral Graphic: Peter Hermes Furian (www.123rf.com)

DEDICATION

To Anthony and Theresa: Two inspiring, fascinating and ever-caring souls who I am so very fortunate to have as my brother and sister in this life.

ACKNOWLEDGMENTS

An enormous thank you to the EP team:
Theresa Cullen – Editor and Marketing Manager;
Michael Cullen – Graphic Designer and Social Media
Manager;
Anthony Costigan – Storyline Consultant,
Anthony E. Walsh – Editor.
Special thanks to family and friends who read draft
versions of the book and shared their very helpful
comments, especially Sharon, Isabel, Clara, Maura,
Paddy, Paul and Andrew.
Also, thanks to Brian MacMahon for help with the Achill
Island research.
For their constant friendship and support, a big thank you
to Rita and Jimmy Murphy, and to Bob Marburg.

CHAPTER 1

The cold breeze stung her face but she hardly noticed. She was more attuned to the feeling of revelry that flowed back and forth between the clans. She glanced up at the crescent moon as it struggled out from behind the nest of clouds, providing welcomed light across the darkened fields. She held on tightly to her young sister's hand. They were almost running now, straining to keep up with the rest of the clan as they strode relentlessly onwards. She could hear the loud whispers all around her. Would the Gods enter the chamber at dawn on a comet of blazing light? Then the dead would breathe again, just as long as the light illuminated the chamber. It would be a bountiful year, with succulent fruits and many sheaves of corn. Sick animals would be healed; the maimed and afflicted would be restored to full strength.

A wave of fear and awe suddenly gripped her, body and soul. She could make out the torches now, carried by thousands of full-blooded men, flanked by women and children, as they huddled together for warmth along the route. She struggled to discern the form that loomed in the distance. At that moment, moonlight slipped free again from its pall, revealing the crystal mansion as it shimmered and sparked in rays of exquisite colour. Almost dizzy with rapture now, she pushed forward, still clinging to her sister's hand.

The officials were gathering in front of the entrance stone. The chief priest and priestess were already inside the sacred circle, welcoming those who were to join them at dawn. Their son, the main attendant, stood beside them, pouring purified water into a small stone bowl that would be used during the ceremony. Her stomach gave a jolt when she saw him gazing into the crowd, searching for a familiar face. Of course he knew she would be here, silently watching his every gesture, ignited by the very sight of him. She lurched forward, still pulling Mel behind her.

She found herself standing in the front row, surrounded by priests and elders, suddenly exposed, uncertain. Mel tugged at her arm, trying to pull her back into obscurity. But it was too late for that now. Her eyes sought those of her secret lover. He took a step forward and her heart pounded wildly. No one must know the truth of their union. There was no open path where their love could flourish, yet she loved this man with all of her being.

The sky suddenly darkened and the air tingled with an invisible force. A loud rumble stunned the entire gathering. Flashes of lightning sent everyone running. In the ensuing chaos Mel bolted free, witless and scared, scampering like a vixen, vanishing out of sight behind the mound.

Rain began to pelt down in torrents. She looked back towards the entrance but it was deserted now. The priests had already sought refuge inside the cairn. She knew with certainty that he would never come to her, no matter how much she needed him. All his sizzling kisses and flaming passion could be so easily extinguished.

She ran through the wet grass that was quickly turning to mud, her hair dripping and her clothing soaked through.

"Mel!" she called. "Mel!"

She was completely alone now. Everyone else had run to seek shelter. She scanned the entire landscape, searching for some sign of life.

From behind a standing stone a stranger emerged.

Mel was clinging to his hand.

"Your sister?" he asked.

"Yes, praise to the Gods," she answered, relief flooding her face.

"You're soaking," he said, as he placed Mel's hand in hers. "My mother and sisters are sheltering just across the field. You'll both be safe there until the storm passes."

For the first time she looked into his eyes. Deep blue eyes like the river in summertime. Kind eyes, like her father's when he was still on earth.

"Who are you?" she asked, as she felt herself thawing out, infused with warmth and comfort. "Who are you?"

CHAPTER 2

She rubbed the sleep from her eyes, then reached across to silence the shrieking alarm. 6.30 am. No doubt it was freezing and pitch black outside. Usually it would have been a bitter struggle to leave her warm cosseted bed. This morning was an exception. She could feel the pent-up excitement tighten its grip on her stomach. The moment was drawing near. This time tomorrow it would be but a memory. The pattern of life: expectation, experience, then memory, with a whole host of feelings thrown in for good measure. She rolled over on her side. There was no light in the room except for the red, glaring digits on the clock.

She had slept little. This kind of experience almost necessitated a review of one's life, at the very least a review of the dwindling year. She recalled fragments of a tangled dream. An anxious, frazzled scene, filled with loneliness and disappointment. A familiar stab pierced her gut. The pain was always greatest on wakening but this morning she was determined to change the pattern. A snippet of the dream still lingered and with it a feeling of safety and hope. Anyway, fate or the Gods had bestowed this momentous gift upon her and she was only too willing to grasp it from the depths of her being. She stretched, then pulled back the eiderdown. It was time to arise.

She always loved the journey to Slane. Out of the city and on the periphery of that rich and fair land. Castles, ancient ruins and old towns with many a tale to tell.

Rolling fields, myths of kings and legends of heroes. All this really appealed to her deep, romantic spirit. She loved the feeling of connection, running her fingers along stonewalls that had been built by other hands, many hundreds or thousands of years before. This was the food of her soul.

A watery moon was slowly dissolving amid the glittering blackness. The sky directly above looked promising. Turning to the east however did little to dispel her nagging doubts. A dark clump of cloud lay stretched across the skyline, foreboding, menacing.

"Come on Gods", she whispered. "Let it be a clear sunrise!"

She yawned and settled back further in her seat. She had never lost her awe of nature with all its power and beauty: wild and ferocious; calm and yielding; innately healing, yet vast and unknowable.

"So, is this the morning when the sun shines into the cave?"

The taxi man glanced at her reflection in the mirror.

"I read about that somewhere recently," he continued. "It's supposed to be a fantastic sight. I've never been to Newgrange myself. I've made a few trips to the interpretative centre all right. It's a big hit with the tourists, especially the Americans and the Dutch. They can't get enough of Irish ruins. I'd like to go there sometime, when I'm not on duty. It'd be good to bring the kids, show them a bit of culture. They probably know more about it than me anyway. They seem to learn a lot more in school nowadays than we ever did. Of course compared to me, you're probably not too long out of school yourself."

She hadn't said much since he'd collected her from Rathmines. She knew she probably seemed aloof and lost in her own world. It was only natural that he was curious. There wouldn't be many who'd be heading for Newgrange, at seven o'clock on a cold winter's morning.

Still, in his job he'd surely met plenty of unusual characters.

"Yes. The twenty-first of December is the Winter Solstice. It's a special morning for Newgrange."

She hadn't learned to drive. Friends and family had always been the drivers. She preferred to walk if her destination was within reasonable distance, or an occasional bus would suffice if need-be. This morning's taxi was a rare event.

"Slane is just around the corner. Then it's about seven kilometres to Newgrange. We should be there by eight."

"Great," she replied. "That leaves plenty of time."

She glanced to the right as the old stone bridge, with arms stretched proudly over the Boyne, glided into view. The sturdy gates of the castle loomed ahead. Slane had everything. Medieval ambience entangled in a web of modern-day legends: the Stones, Dylan, Springsteen. Hot summer days, electrifying rock, dancing barefoot on sunburnt grass. Good times. But then with lightning speed her mind threw up a series of troubling visions: a couple strolling on a beach, the girl's long skirt clinging to her bare wet legs; two dreamy lovers engrossed in a warm embrace; a pair of dark, sparkling eyes pulling her inwards, promising to unlock the very riddle of life.

The taxi-driver veered right from Slane. It was quite a narrow road. Fields, hedges, and tall naked trees lined the route. She noted a signpost for Knowth, pointing to the right.

"We turn left up here for Newgrange," he said.

A few hundred yards later there was another signpost. This time for Dowth, with the arrow pointing left: the completion of the trilogy.

The darkness was now fading rapidly. The sky's cloak was a patchwork of blues and greys of every shade. Except for the car in front, the road was deserted.

She kept her eyes peeled for sudden changes in the

sky. She was suddenly giddy with excitement, mixed with a tinge of apprehension. A whole range of thoughts sprang up as she surveyed the landscape. "What must this morning have meant to the original builders? Did people travel great distances to be at Newgrange on the solstice? Would they have gathered in their thousands outside *Bru na Boinne*—the mansion of the Boyne?"

She could easily imagine the gradual procession from nearby villages, walking through dark, freezing fields, filled with the same excitement and hope that she now felt—five-thousand-years later. Finally they would assemble outside the cairn, straining to catch sight of those who would be entering the mound, praying that the sun would light up the chamber and breathe new life into a recently departed mother, brother, husband or lover. For this would have been the ultimate proof that a time of great bounty was in store for all.

The Boyne monuments were revered as sacred sites for thousands of years. She knew the legends almost by heart. Ancient folklore associated Newgrange with the legendary Tuatha de Danann, the ancient rulers of Ireland. From earliest times it was believed that Newgrange had been erected as a burial place for the chief of the gods, the Dagda, and his three sons. The Dagda was noted for his cauldron of plenty that no one could leave without being satisfied, and for his harp that could play three airs: the sleep strain, the grief strain, and the laughter strain. One of his sons, Aonghus, known as the great God of love, was the product of a secret union between the Dagda and Boann, the river Boyne. Aonghus, so the legend goes, asked his father if he could have Newgrange for one day and one night. The Dagda granted his wish, but Aonghus tricked him by saying that one day and one night meant forever, and so he remained in possession.

The last bend in the road. She caught sight of a white gleaming curve. Another moment and it would come into full view. She held her breath. There it stood in all its magnificence, mysterious and proud on a sloping ridge of earth. The white quartz surface glinted, jewel-like, in the light of two torches, then curved into darkness. The standing stones of the great circle projected their primal power. Only the chosen few would cross the threshold at dawn. The famous entrance-stone with its mysterious spirals was barely visible in the dim light.

"Thanks. Will that cover it? No, keep the change. Thanks again."

"Enjoy the big occasion." He smiled as she slid out into the cold morning air. "Hope it's worth it."

"It will be," she said with an air of certainty.

CHAPTER 3

She wasn't the first to arrive. Four cars were parked in front of the wire fence. She thanked her lucky stars the morning was fine. The cold presented little problem as she had come well prepared, with several layers of fleece and two pairs of woolly socks. This wasn't her first solstice vigil at Newgrange. Two years previously she had set out with four fellow pilgrims, her old college friends, Jim and Niamh, her workmate, Lynn, and her cousin, Mike. That morning had been black and spilling rain. Niamh had brought a Clannad album and Lynn had chipped in with Anuna. They had sung along as sheets of rain enveloped them, something about winter fire being beautiful. Jim had been the instigator.

"Why not go to Newgrange for sunrise on December twenty-first? Wouldn't that be a great way to bring some depth and spirituality back into the festive season?"

Marion had jumped at the chance. As a child, Christmas had meant lots of presents, shiny tinsel and baubles, dazzling Christmas lights, all kinds of delicious goodies, a time of family, excitement and fun. There had been the odd trip to church to visit the crib and to listen to the carol singers. Now Christmas meant avoiding work parties, shopping in crowded streets and days of rest and recuperation. There was little spiritual significance.

Since her first visit to Newgrange and her reading of old Irish folktales and legends, a new meaning for this time of year had begun to emerge. For countless generations the Winter Solstice had been a time of celebration. For those ancient people in their completely natural environment it marked the end of the long dark days, the freezing cold nights and the hard barren earth. It was the rebirth of the sun. What better reason to rejoice?

"I know I'll find it really hard to get up so early, Jim, but sure, it will be a great adventure. As you know, I've had my name on the Newgrange list for eight years now. In two years' time it'll be my long-awaited turn to enter the chamber and to feel the sun's rays filling the inner sanctum with its golden light. I know it doesn't happen every year. Sometimes the sky is too cloudy and the rays aren't strong enough to enter the roof-box. I've had several dreams of being there on that morning, of witnessing the stunning event. I only pray these dreams are prophetic and that I'll actually be lucky enough to see the full spectacle, in all its glory."

"It'll be a real sneak-preview for you then." Jim smiled at his friend's obvious delight. "It'll be a thrill for me just to be there on the solstice, following in the footsteps of our Neolithic ancestors. That will be something I'll certainly savour."

Jim was her best friend. Jim knew her better than anyone. They had gone through all kinds of experiences together and through it all they'd remained friends. She knew with certainty that she'd always love him and that this feeling was mutual. But it was brotherly love. Long ago she'd thought there was a chance of romance, but it was not to be. Jim was gay. He was also sensitive, creative, and deeply caring, with a sharp probing mind and a natural leaning towards the mystical.

On that morning, all their singing and high jinx had turned to wailing. Jim had rounded the last bend when he was waved into the ditch by the Gardaí.

"No entrance to Newgrange this morning. Sorry folks, unless you have an official pass I can't let you through. There's a VIP visiting the site. You won't be admitted to the grounds until ten o'clock."

She could still feel the bitter disappointment. Denied access to an ancient sacred site, because of some VIP! They protested vehemently but to no avail. There was nothing for it but to retreat to the nearest restaurant for breakfast and lick their wounds. Later that morning Lynn rang *Ryan on the Radio* to vent her annoyance and she'd actually been interviewed over the airwaves. Along with Jim, she had written protest letters to the Heritage Centre. The verdict: there was no way to beat the system. Just grin and bear it.

She pushed a rebel strand of hair away from her eyes. This morning would be different. She felt the crisp envelope in her right-hand pocket through her gloved fingers. The official pass was in her hand. The long-awaited experience was within her grasp.

8.10. Darkness was fading fast. The entire sky was awaiting its cosmic king. Not too long now for the sun to give the earth its kiss of life. She walked towards the entrance. Access to the site was only permitted through a wooden gate at the side. The rest of the site was protected by a wire fence. Three tall, fair-haired men aged somewhere in their thirties were standing at the fence, staring at the monument, probably theorising as to what purpose it had originally been built for. From their accents they sounded German. Of course, Newgrange was now world renowned, as the taxi-driver had reminded her, no longer a local affair.

Two men and one woman, all carrying cameras and heavy bags, were already at the entrance. A small fair-haired woman, dressed in a striking red coat, with folder and pen in hand, was speaking to them from behind the gate.

"Yes, your name is here, Michael. You too, Teresa. And I've already met you, David. I won't be admitting anyone to the site until 8.45, so you've plenty of time yet. It's a good morning so let's hope we'll all be in luck.

Yesterday was rather overcast so we didn't see anything. I'm told by the experts that today is touch and go, but we'll see."

The media people seemed disappointed with the news and walked away, chatting, towards the fence.

Marion walked towards the gate where the red-coated lady was still standing.

"Hello, I'm Nuala. You're very welcome to Newgrange on this auspicious morning. Is your name on the official list?"

"Yes, I hope so. I'm Marion Nielson." She held out her small, gloved hand.

Nuala consulted her folder. "Oh yes, Marion. You're here all right. Have you ever been here for the Solstice before? You seem a bit familiar."

"Last year I was here, but not in the chamber. Even just being on the site was a great experience. This year it'll be a dream come true to actually be inside the cairn at dawn."

"Well, I certainly hope you enjoy it. Maybe you'll even get the full feature, though nothing is ever guaranteed. We won't be moving inside until around 8.45. Dawn is set for 8.58 so don't worry, you won't miss a thing. It's a bit cloudy at the moment to the East, but let's hope it'll burn itself off. Just relax and absorb the atmosphere."

Then Nuala of the Red Coat walked briskly up the pathway towards the visitor's enclosure.

Left alone again, Marion moved to the fence, fingering the wire through her velvet gloves. The cairn was magnificent, perfectly positioned on elevated land: a stately sentinel for all the world to see. Whatever its purpose, it had long-since captured her imagination and cast a binding spell around her soul.

Last year she had stood there, perhaps in the exact spot, waiting to experience her first solstice on the site. She had been envious then of the line-up of media people and the two politicians who had been given privileged passes. They had seen nothing that morning. The sun's rays had failed to reach the crowded chamber.

For her, dawn had been a magical moment. She had stood with her back supported by the ancient kerb stones as the first rays of sunlight burst upon the horizon. Streaks of golden light had shot up from the east, exploding fireworks of unearthly beauty. Within seconds, cascading clouds had stifled the sparks, creating a palette of silver, grey-blue and pale yellow.

Forty to fifty expectant visitors had witnessed the event. An eerie silence hovered over those assembled. The moment of dawn, the mysterious standing stones, the majestic Boyne flowing below, the earth's green mantle stretching for miles as far as the eye could see. A young girl next to her had tried to light a candle to mark the moment but the breeze had been too strong. A group of friends hugged and kissed. Their words floated on the breeze to where she was standing.

"Happy New Year!"

"Let the light of Newgrange guide you throughout the coming year."

She remembered the American family. The mother with her arms wrapped around her teenage daughter, shielding her from the cold; the father shaking his head in disbelief.

"Wow! This is amazing, Rita. There's some kind of supernatural presence here all right. Can you feel that energy? You can almost touch it. I can really feel the hairs standing up on the back of my neck. What a great idea to come here?"

All that seemed like light years away. It was part of a different reality, in many ways a different life. Last year she had not been alone. He had been here at her side. It had been a huge surprise that he'd agreed to accompany her. That had been a big bonus. He had revelled in the experience too in his own way. She could still hear the echo of their voices on the wind...

"Well, Peter, to me the three entwined spirals represent body, mind and spirit. Maybe this is what the three parts of the shamrock once meant to the Irish, before St. Patrick introduced his father, son and Holy Ghost. It's a symbol of immortality. The body and the mind are the two spirals below. These are the aspects of the person that will fade and die. The spiral above is the spirit. This has no beginning and no end."

He shook his head.

"No, Marion, that doesn't fit for me."

That was no surprise. If the day ever dawned when he didn't wince at the mention of 'spirit' there would be shock waves reverberating around the earth for years.

"Well, what's your theory then?" she asked. "Why were the monuments of Knowth, Dowth and Newgrange originally constructed?"

Now he was in his element. He grinned like a little kid who has just been presented with a much-coveted toy. Of course she knew he had a bag-full of theories. But it always fascinated her to hear his latest one.

"Okay then!" He looked towards the enigma, which had puzzled and intrigued a host of generations. "Newgrange is a fertility symbol. The narrow winding passage is the birth canal which finally widens out into the chamber–the megalithic womb. During the Winter Solstice the sun's rays penetrate the roof-box–the vagina. This solar shaft of light, pushing its way upwards until it reaches the chamber, is a symbol of fertilisation. This was a concept of cosmic sexual intercourse, a symbol of the natural forces inherent in nature which every individual could understand. Perhaps these people did worship the sun as a deity. The chamber was the burial place for a privileged few, perhaps kings or rulers. What more powerful ritual than for the sun to penetrate the stone womb and to breathe new life into the ashes and bones of the dead?"

She could still see his dark eyes sparkling as he gazed towards the cairn. The breeze was strong that morning so he'd kept running his fingers through his hair.

"These people were mainly farmers." He had turned to survey the rolling fertile fields. "Their most important need was water, hence their location next to the river Boyne. This was a perfect location—rich arable soil, good grazing land, with access to fuel and building materials. The sun was the source of all of nature's gifts. Without the sun there would be no light, no heat, no food and hence no life. The sun became a God to these early people, the giver of life, infinitely magnificent in the variety of colours manifested by its light. Observing the sky and the sun's position was vital for man's survival. Through constant observation, patterns in nature began to emerge. Day was seen to follow night, season followed season. Then there were the solstices. The length that the sun was in the sky peaked at mid-summer and was least at mid-winter. The concept of time, the growth and decay of plants, the periods of plenty and scarcity, all were determined by the movement of the sun. The Winter Solstice marked the end of the old year and the beginning of the new. Is it little wonder then, that the monuments built by these people placed the sun as the central focal point of their whole community?"

He paused to catch his breath, well satisfied. In a moment he was off again, weaving more intricate theories. There was no one quite like Peter when he was in this frame of mind.

"The spirals may represent the triple aspect of the Goddess: youth, maturity and old-age. Remember that the sun has always been a male symbol. The earth, the cairn and the stone basins found inside the chamber of Newgrange are all female symbols. Surely the Goddess had a vital role to play in the fertility celebrations? The

Egyptians, the American Indians and the Aborigines all have a similar folklore. At Newgrange we are confronted by the same universal themes: sex and death. Five-thousand-years later, the themes which grip human consciousness are the same, the ultimate mystery of life."

She had been spellbound by his words. Not for the first time she had wondered where he had come from: The Valley of the Kings, perhaps? That morning she had felt truly blessed to have found a man who could excite her at every level of her being. She smiled up at him, watching the way the breeze played with his dark hair. She would have loved to hold him then, to press her face against his chest, to feel him caressing her. If this was a sacred fertility site, then why couldn't she kiss the man she loved, on the very feast of the ancient ritual? But no, he was never one for public displays of affection.

"Mm, very interesting, Peter. It actually ties in well with a book I'm reading, based on the Goddess, Brigid. She was known as the triple Goddess: the great mother, lover, and maiden. Before the legend of Brigid was watered down by the early Christians she was associated with the Tuatha de Dannan and revered as the daughter of the Dagda. She was a sun Goddess. Her famous crosses are similar to swastikas found in ancient cultures all over the world and are symbols of the sun."

She had revelled in these discussions, where mind fused with mind, in much the same way that she'd delighted in making love, in feeling their bodies moving, melting, slowly disintegrating.

"According to legend, Brigid was born at sunrise." She loved the way he stroked his chin when he was deeply focused. She had his full attention then.

"Her breath could revive the spirit of the dead," she continued. "She was noted as a healer, a midwife, a law-maker and a patron of poets. Her feast day, February First, derives from an ancient festival of the Goddess, which culminated in a ritual mating ceremony to bring new life to the community. Her symbols were the sacred cow, the giver of milk and nourishment, and the serpent, the representation of rebirth and rejuvenation. Imagine three coiled serpents, each one representing an aspect of the Goddess? This wouldn't be too far from the famous spirals, would it now?"

He smiled and nodded his approval. He was impressed. "If we keep agreeing like this there won't be any hope for us," he laughed.

He even agreed to walk three times around the mound. He may have been commemorating the ancient fertility rites of the Goddess. For her, Newgrange was still a place of deep spiritual significance, a meeting of two worlds, a timeless quest and an aspiration for immortality.

There was a time when nothing had mattered but to be with him. No previous experience could give her a handle on this one. Withdrawal symptoms invariably followed their partings. Excruciating pain was always the result of a quarrel, an insensitive word, a thoughtless deed. And there had been plenty of these towards the end.

"How can I stop the thoughts, much less the feelings?" she asked herself for the zillionth time. But somehow it was vital to recall every detail, not to block the memories. The release of pain was part of her process of healing. The day she didn't feel pain she'd know she had either died or been reborn. It was imperative that she piece together the jigsaw, even though there were pieces she may never have in her possession. She desperately needed to understand what had happened over the last five years. How much had she actually changed? She wanted to learn so she'd never make the same mistakes again. Sure, she couldn't live without making mistakes. The only thing she knew for certain was that she'd never go through this amount of pain again. This was the breaking of the shell, the disintegration of her innocence.

She raised her head and stared at the beckoning icon. Not many people were given the chance to enter a sanctuary, to take part in an ancient, sacred ritual of rebirth. Today was her lifeline, her rebirth, her renewal. She would grasp this opportunity with all of her strength. It was time to exorcise her demons, to separate the jewels from the rhinestones and enter a new phase, enhanced by experience. This was about as positive as she could be.

CHAPTER 4

Her mind drifted back to yet another world and another experience. The first time she'd met him...

"Hi Marion, this is Peter, an old friend. Peter, this is Marion."

"Hello Marion."

"Hi Peter."

The most striking feature had been the eyes: black, proud, sparkling. Dark hair, a sensuous mouth, sallow skin, about six feet tall. Statistics, mere physical characteristics. She could still see him looking at her, a long look, an intimate look. Even from the first moment there had been a recognition; a strange energy, an intensity, a chemistry. She'd read about this kind of thing. Certainly she had only experienced it once – with Peter.

She liked to collect beautiful things: works of art, sculpture, strained glass and tapestries. She enjoyed being surrounded by beauty. Yet she could never understand some people's obsession with human physical attributes. Sure, there had to be a physical attraction, but there are millions of pretty faces, perfectly shaped, tastefully clad bodies. It was the essence, the soul, the thoughts and the feelings, the many intricate, often painfully woven layers of experiences, values, beliefs and dreams. This is the core of each unique life.

The party had been at Anne's place. Niamh had first introduced her to Anne when they were at college. Anne had gone to school with Peter's sister and seemed to know the family well, hence his presence at the gathering. It was Friday evening. She had been in two minds whether or not to go. She wouldn't know many people there. She felt tired after a long hard week, interviewing a sample of the populace about their work conditions. Anne's flat was in Ranelagh, just down the road from hers and the music was usually good at her parties. She decided to give it a go. If it was a bore she could always slip away early, unnoticed.

Everything was in full swing when she arrived. There were people everywhere, dancing, chatting, lying on floors, drinking, kissing. She'd never been a lover of wild parties. Small, intimate gatherings were her forte. Anne grabbed her arm as soon as she opened the door and shouted above the din.

"Marion! It's great you could come. Give me a hug! It's mad in here. Angie's dancing and Tina's here too, somewhere. Oh, there's someone I'd like you to meet. He's different. I think you'll like him. He just arrived a few minutes before you. He's alone. Follow me."

He was leaning against the wall sipping a can of beer, a cigarette dangling between his fingers.

"Can I get you a drink?" he asked. "There's quite a variety to choose from. Anne is a good hostess."

"Just some mineral water, thanks."

She watched as he crossed the room. He was lean and tanned, and he moved with an elegance, a kind of animal grace. He seemed to be very much at home with his physicalness. Cool and confident, without a bone of self-consciousness.

He returned carrying a bottle of Ballygowan in one hand and a large can in the other.

"So Marion, what's your taste in music?" He lowered himself to the floor and she did likewise.

"Well, a mixture of rock, blues, folk and some '60s sounds. And I like that Floyd beat. I wouldn't have bothered stirring out tonight only I know Anne's taste in music. I'm not a drinker, so unless the music and of course the company is good I'm not inclined to attend parties."

His eyes lit up at the mention of Floyd.

"Yeah, right on! Put it there, Marion."

He held up his can for her to clink.

"So you're a '60s rocker? And I presume you don't exclude the '70s? Ok, so what about Zeppelin, old Fleetwood Mac, and Deep Purple? They're definitely in my all-time top twenty."

They'd chatted for hours. She couldn't remember the exact twists and turns the conversation had taken. It could have included the meaning of life, Viking Dublin, Socrates and Plato, the Beatles, the films of Steve McQueen, French impressionist artists, Pharaohs and pyramids, Tolkien's incredible creations, Ireland's chances in the world cup, the poetry of W. B Yeats, Jimi Hendrix and Woodstock; life, the universe and everything. There was no end to the fertile pastures of his mind. Her imaginative spark was always well and truly ignited, whenever she was with Peter.

He had told her something of his background, even on that first evening. Thinking back now they must have been surrounded by kissing couples, crazy dancers and at times deafening drumbeats but they had been all but oblivious to the ensuing din. The soldering of hearts, minds and souls had instantly begun.

He came from a strange yet fascinating family. There was a feminist mother; a father who travelled the world sailing yachts; a sister whom he adored, who taught history and English. There was an older brother, the outcast of the family, who worked in a bank and had married a born-again Christian. Then there was Tom, the youngest boy. He fancied himself as the next Jim Morrison; he sang and played guitar with The Asylum.

Peter had a natural ease around women. This must have been due to his closeness with his mother and sister.

But there was yet another female in his life: his girlfriend, Jean. That was the bombshell. He had been living with Jean for eight years.

Marion could still recall the sinking sensation in the pit of her stomach when he revealed the latter. At the time she had shrugged her shoulders and tried to ease herself away from his magnetic charm. She had just met the guy. He was a stranger. He wasn't part of her life so it didn't really matter where he lived or who he lived with. Somehow it hadn't been that simple. Everything about him intrigued her. From that first evening it had been impossible to walk away.

There had never been any guessing games with Peter. He was straight, refreshingly open, up front. He had no problem talking about his past. He'd told her he was something of a loner as a child, isolated at school because other kids sensed a difference. He had been painfully thin, with no interest in physical sports. He had created his own science lab at home where he'd messed around with basic chemicals and concoctions, experimenting, questioning. He'd written poetry sparingly and he'd filled many a notebook full of stories, experiences and observations. He read profusely, yet carefully: biographies, history, anthropology, mythology, modern classics, philosophy, and anything else that fired his imagination. His sister shared some of his inner world, though much remained closed, out of bounds.

He had grown up in the height of the '60s, where idealism and social revolution were rife. His idol was John Lennon. He had no God, except Eric Clapton. Music, he said, was his religion. His mother had been too involved in political campaigns and social reform to bother with "some hairy old man in the sky", who had nothing better to do than to pass judgment on how people chose to live their lives. The only labels he attached to himself were those of realist and atheist.

"Well, if you've never met an atheist before, here's

the real McCoy. There is no such thing as a God. It's a man-made concept, a figment of the imagination, like ghosts and ghouls, fairies and Santa clause. It derives from man's infancy, before we understood the workings of the cosmos. God represents man's greatest ignorance. God was the super-being who rewarded nations that obeyed him and destroyed those that didn't. God was a way of evading responsibility for each person's own life and destiny. If you ever pick up a history book or a newspaper you can't help seeing the amount of appalling crimes which have been carried out in *a Gadda da Vida.* When I die, that's it! Is that such a frightening thought? Is it too much for the poor ego to take? While I'm here I aim to experience life, to create a meaningful existence, to have a damn great time and still to be fully responsible for my own actions. My mind is my God, Marion. Intelligence and reason are the keys to all things!"

He loved to challenge, to dare people to question their most cherished beliefs. He readily admitted a degree of arrogance. At times she saw this clearly enough. He never suffered fools. He certainly had a rare confidence in the brilliance of his mind. He was the only person she'd ever met who had a photographic memory—for people, places, faces, dates, and facts.

"And here I was thinking you were called after Saint Peter," she teased.

"There's a fat chance of that, about the same probability that your name derives from your mother's love of Robin Hood and his spirited maid!"

"It was my grandmother's name, actually," she laughed.

"Peter was my grandfather," he grinned.

Then it was back to more serious matters.

"I suppose you're another God-lover."

He paused to sip his beer and then gave her a boyish grin to take the edge from his last remark.

"People who spend time talking with me often end

up with a pain in their head. They can't seem to keep up with the pace. I hope you've a little more stamina, Marion."

"I do feel there is a God–is that a problem?"

She was known herself to revel in verbal challenges. Not many people talked about such things, though everyone had to ask these questions at some time in their lives. Where have I come from? What am I doing here? Where am I going? No one could surely escape the urge to wonder what this existence was all about. Life made pretty certain of that. She remembered, as a child of seven or eight, beginning to form these same questions. She had just become conscious of herself as a separate person, as a human being who had a limited life span.

"What is God to me?"

Her eyes danced and her face glowed with an inner light.

"God is the answer to the mystery of life, to the patterns and intelligence inherent in nature. Do you really believe the whole workings of the universe are just some accident? That certainly isn't a reasonable explanation. To me, God is a feeling, the source of life, the connection between all living beings. God is energy which can never be created or destroyed. I am part of God. My body will one day turn to dust, like the petals on the rose, which curl, wither, and fall. My spirit, however, is invincible, eternal."

She could sense his excitement. His eyes sparkled as he gave her an irresistible smile.

"At least you haven't mentioned religion or dubious rules that you were told to obey since you were an infant. But how can you believe in something you can't see?"

Now she was in her element.

"The most powerful energy on earth is feeling. Love, hatred, fear, sadness, joy, guilt, wonder, anger, jealousy, excitement, frustration–the list is long. How can we ever define, dissect or capture any of these feelings? You talk of reason and intelligence, but we also need to acknowledge our feelings, or we wouldn't be human. We catch glimpses of people's feelings through their behaviour, but feelings are not tangible, something we can touch or hold. They don't have a visible colour or shape, unless of course you're psychic, but they are real. To me, God is a feeling: A feeling that I am here on this earth to experience and to learn, to grow and to fulfil as much of my potential as is humanly possible. A feeling that I have always existed and that I always will. This isn't about religion or rules. It's about my personal search for meaning and coherence in my own life."

She was pleased with the way she'd expressed herself. She took a sip of her Ballygowan. Peter tried to persuade her to take a glass of Guinness, for the experience, in much the same way he challenged her to forget about God, even for one day. He seemed intrigued by her innocence, by her lack of worldly experience. He was only five years older but he had done so many things in his life. Before Jean, he'd had two previous relationships. He'd smoked opium with the tribesmen on the mountaintops of Northern Thailand. He'd taken LSD in California at a week-long rock festival. He'd even introduced the Greek natives to Jameson whiskey while sunbathing naked on the beaches of Kos. He had worked as a cook, a gardener, and had sold crafts at a market during the summer he'd lived in London. There were, of course, many differences between them, but Marion could only see the similarities for the two years they'd remained friends.

"But why does there have to be a meaning?" He took a sip of beer and wiped his lips with the back of his hand. For hours these conversations had blazed, at fever pitch.

"You have a need to feel you are eternal," he continued. "The thought of dying is too frightening for you. The thought of losing someone and never seeing that person again is too scary. So your mind has created a defense, a cocoon; a place where you can hide to protect you from the stark realities of life. But I can understand that. It's a safety valve to give you consolation in times of pain. For me, there's no such cushion. There is just experience and living for this moment."

They always agreed to differ during those hours, days, weeks, months, and years of razor-edged theorising and debating. Of course, nothing could ever be proven. God, how she loved every minute of it! There was a continual stripping away of superfluous layers, of old values and beliefs she had been indoctrinated with, by family, school, church and state. All this heavy baggage was gradually shed. In the early days there was a freshness, a breathing in of cool clear mountain air: pure, unspoilt and intoxicating.

Peter worked as a computer consultant for a software firm on Wellington Quay. He liked his work, maintaining the computer system, testing new software, investigating 'bugs', and documenting solutions. In his spare time he was a freelance artist. He had designed a few book-covers, including one for a feminist publication, and two CD sleeves. He had also done a few advertisement assignments. Mainly he sketched for fun. He had formally studied neither computers nor art, yet he seemed to excel at both. He learned through reading and experience, through trial and error. He believed in seizing all opportunities that came his way.

"Everyone makes mistakes, Marion. Everyone gets hurt in this game of life." He'd shrugged his shoulders and laughed. "So what? The fickle fortunes of life turn on a dime. So why not spin that dime and see what destiny holds!"

He trusted himself and his abilities above all else.

"Trust in oneself," he'd once said, "and not in some invisible God, is my most basic philosophy."

Marion told him something of her own life. She had been reared in Curracloe, a small village about eight miles from Wexford town. The main attraction had been the glorious miles of beautiful golden beach. As a child, she hadn't realised it was ranked among the finest in Europe. To her it had been a haven, a wild and free sanctuary from the problems of school and the uncertainty of teenage years. In summer it was packed with tourists, many of whom had come from the cities, to melt, unwind and heal in the warm, blue sea under the blazing, yellow sun. At night-time she often walked with her brother, Greg, along the seashore, enthralled by the silver moonlight sparkling and dancing on the ethereal waves. In winter the beach was deserted. The water would then be icy cold to the touch and the whole sky silvery grey.

There were days when the huge, bellowing waves lashed out like some poor tormented beast. She loved to sit on the grassy bank, her hair sprayed out all around her, staring out to sea, surrounded by the roar of the waves and the screaming of the wind. She could feel an enormous, awesome power emanating from this place. It was all natural energy. For hours she often sat, hypnotised by the sheer magic and beauty of the perfect combination of sea, sky and sand. This is where she was closest to unravelling the truth of her existence. This is where she felt nearest to God. Here she was supremely spiritual, and yet so physically and sensually alive.

She had left home six years previously to attend college in Dublin. She had always been close to her family and still returned every few weekends. The psychology degree she'd studied at UCD had been a major disappointment because it was so theoretical. She had really enjoyed college though, especially the social life. There had been a great variety of people to connect with. Her closest friends, Jim and Niamh, had both been in her class. There had also been the odd date to bring a bit of novelty and spice to the week. There was one guy in particular, John, who she had fallen in love with. They had known each other as friends for several months before the big bang had exploded in her head. Then she started to feel this strange passion for him. He obviously noticed the change and asked her out. It was nice while it lasted. It had really been quite low key and hadn't involved a great deal of sexual connection. Soon after, John left college for a job in Cork. They wrote to each other and met a few times. In the end, he told her it wouldn't work and she hadn't seen him since. It was very upsetting at the time and there had been plenty of tears shed, but by now she was well over it.

When she first met Peter she was doing research and preparing questionnaires as part of a social study's programme. She had always been fascinated by people, hence her choice of career. She had a profound belief that change is always possible in people's lives, no matter where they have come from, or what difficulties or pain they have experienced. Trust for her was in the human psyche's ability to heal itself. She hadn't found her niche just yet. She was awaiting inspiration.

Her childhood had in many ways paralleled Peter's. His closeness with his mother and sister mirrored her own, with her father and brother. She, too, had remained aloof from other children, preferring the company of like-minded adults. She had written poetry and songs as a kid. She had fuelled her vivid imagination with books and dreams of history, art, legends, and classic tales. Her favourite book had been *Wuthering Heights*. The artists she loved were the Pre-Raphaelites, especially Rossetti. The poets she preferred were Hardy, Yeats and Poe. All were rich in atmosphere, deep, dark, passionate and romantic, where mystical, unseen forces played a fateful hand in the shaping of mortal destiny...

Marion was suddenly awakened from her reverie.

"Hi, there! We're just wondering if it'll be possible for us to get access to the site this morning. We don't have official passes but we'd like to be on the grounds at dawn to celebrate the solstice."

Two striking girls with English accents had just got out of an old Beetle car, and were making their way towards the fence where Marion was still standing. One of the girls had long strawberry-blonde hair, loosely tied with a blue silk scarf. Her hazel eyes were set in a flawlessly-carved face. She wore a saffron-coloured jacket over a long, multi-coloured dress. Dozens of silver bangles jingle-jangled every time she moved. The second girl had jet-black hair to her waist, all combed out around her shoulders. Her eyes were lined with mascara, and her lips and nails were blood red. She was dressed in a long green coat, a colourful tie-dyed skirt and black suede boots. A golden sun-pendant hung from a silver string around her neck. They could both have walked straight out of a pre-Raphaelite painting. Perhaps it was Lizzie Siddal and Jane Burden, Rossetti's models and lovers, who had just materialised in front of her?

"Yes. I'm sure you'll be allowed on the site for sunrise. I was here last year and I had no problem," Marion replied.

The two girls smiled and gave a sigh of relief.

"We're so glad to hear that. We've travelled over from London. A friend of ours said we'd have no trouble exploring the grounds of Newgrange. Hi, I'm Layla, by the way, and this is Jade."

The black-haired girl introduced them both.

"Hello, I'm Marion."

They shook hands and Layla continued.

"It really does look incredible. I've always wanted to visit Newgrange. It's older than Stonehenge, by about five-hundred-years, isn't it? I've read a book about the chamber being completely lit up at this time of year. Boy, I'd give anything to see that."

"You'll both be allowed inside after the main feature is over. I'm really very honoured to have the chance to be in the cairn at dawn. I've waited eight years, but I know it'll be more than worth it."

The girls gasped and Marion could see their envy.

"It's a once in a life time experience, I'll bet." Jade, the strawberry-blonde, chimed in. "We've been to Stonehenge a few times for the Summer Solstice. You can't really get near the place most years though with the amount of cops. They've really ruined it for the ordinary people who just want to celebrate the longest day in the ancient tradition. Something so beautiful and sacred has been turned into a battleground. I actually prefer visiting Stonehenge when there's nothing major happening there. My boyfriend is from Salisbury. We drive up every once in a while just to soak up the energy from the earth and the huge mysterious stones. It's a fantastic place. Have you ever been there?"

"No. But I'd love to go there sometime. The experts say it was originally built to observe the movement of the sun and the moon, is that right?"

Marion had always wanted to visit Stonehenge. She'd planned to go there with Jim next summer. They'd also invited Conor, another college friend, but they had been horrified when he'd described the sacred site as, "a few scattered stones lying in a field." So that had put an end to the invitation. He had never really been on the same wavelength though, so it hadn't come as much of a shock.

Layla, the black-haired girl, was speaking again.

"Well, I've no doubt that the megalithic stones of Stonehenge are living symbols of the ancient sacred tradition and religion of the pre-Celtic people. Whoever built them had a full understanding of the solstices, the equinoxes and the sun's eclipses. The ancient people lived in harmony with the cosmic rhythms and natural cycles. I really feel we're going back to that time now, the Age of Aquarius and all that. Isn't that what the New Age is all about? Rediscovering all the knowledge and wisdom that ancient cultures lived by. So much has been damaged or destroyed by our own culture through greed and ignorance. I admit I'm an idealist but people have got to change their attitudes to the earth, and to learn to respect and nurture it before it's too late."

It was a sentiment that in many ways Marion shared. There was no time to answer though as Nuala of the Red Coat had just opened the gate, probably to answer queries from newcomers. The girls said they'd talk again later after they'd got official permission to enter the site. And with that, they shook their radiant manes like two rare thoroughbreds and pranced towards the gate, resplendent in the early morning light.

CHAPTER 5

8.15. The cold was beginning to seep into her bones. She stamped her feet and strode along by the fence. There was still plenty of time to gather up a few more pieces of the jigsaw…

He had taken her number that evening, making it clear he'd like to meet her again, as a friend. There had never been anything dishonest about Peter. He didn't give her false hopes. He was living with Jean but he'd like to make a new friend. She had hoped he'd call. She already had three male friends who she met at least a few times a month. Jim was gay. Anto was living with Eva. Conor was great fun to be with but she wasn't in the least bit attracted to him. She had often questioned herself why she seemed to have so many of these platonic friendships. Men often told her she was pretty but unless she could connect with a man mentally she really had no interest in getting in any deeper. She had always secretly yearned for a soulmate.

The difference between a friend and a lover had often puzzled her. Was there a difference? At the time she met Peter she believed they could be friends. Later she realised that when you are completely besotted by someone then you are only waiting for that smouldering friendship to explode into love. Of course, every relationship has its needs and its responsibilities but once the sexual dimension enters the picture, an eruption to equal Mount Vesuvius occurs. Experience is the only way to discover the truth.

Peter rang her a few days later at work. He sounded warm and friendly. He chatted about the latest Dire Straits' album he'd bought, and the film he'd gone to the evening before. He asked if she'd like to meet for coffee in Bewley's. She was delighted and arranged to meet him after work. Even on that first evening there was no awkwardness. After an hour in Bewley's they moved onto The Norseman, and then to The Chancery Inn. She could still remember most of that evening. He had sat there holding court, savouring his Guinness and inhaling his beloved Silk Cut. She had been entranced, sipping her Ballygowan. The entire evening had floated by, sharing experiences, laughing at the absurdity of life, debating the meaning of existence. Occasionally they'd tuned in to the Irish ballads being played by the musicians at the back of the pub. It was almost midnight before she got home. The pattern for the early days of their friendship had been set. They would call each other most weeks and meet up after work, at the very least every fortnight.

She was surprised how little detail she could recall about those early days. It was mainly the feeling of excitement, of a new confidence in herself which she'd never known before and the overall sense of fun. Peter brought her to places she'd never heard of. Night-clubs where bands played brilliant cover versions of groups like, The Rolling Stones, Fleetwood Mac and The Doors. Sometimes they'd head for a blues session. Her favourites were The Mary Stokes Band, The Legendary Hoods and The International Blues Band. There were nights when she felt so intoxicated by the music that she just had to dance. Usually the clubs were packed and there was hardly room to swing a cat. This didn't deter her though. Sometimes he'd dance too, when he had a few drinks too many, jigging around, shaking his head from side to side, shuffling his feet, clicking his fingers.

"We're really getting into the groove now, man!"

He'd tilt his head back and laugh. "Let it all hang out, Marion. Move to the beat of the blues. Let it fill your head and move your soul. And for those who don't have a soul, let it move your feet, man!"

She never wanted to go home, to leave him for another week. Within a few weeks she was head over heels in love. She thought about him first thing in the morning, invariably last thing at night, and he even managed to make regular appearances in her dreams. Friends asked her what the story was. They were naturally protective of her, glad she was having a good time but just waiting for the bubble to burst. Lynn was the first to ask the six million dollar question.

"Why is he meeting you, Marion, and spending so much time with you when he's living with someone else?"

She didn't know the answer to this herself. He wanted a friend. That's all he ever said. He had many acquaintances but only a handful of friends. He said he really liked her. Especially he liked her intelligence, her sensitivity and the way she hadn't been tainted or hardened by the sorrows of life. Sometimes he teased her ideals and values but she could feel deep down he admired them. He liked people of integrity, real people, people with minds and hearts and guts, and the occasional soul. He had no time for cheap sentiment or dishonesty, only for truth. Once he mentioned that having a friend who you were also attracted to added an extra twist to the friendship. This made her stomach jolt and her face flush. It was more than she could ever hope for.

Usually when they met after work he'd be dressed in a dark, grey suit, a snow-white shirt and a skinny, blue tie. He looked incredibly attractive she always thought. It would have suited him better though to wear a calfskin tunic and frayed trousers, to dab war-paint streaks all over his face and to don a feathered headdress. He could easily have passed for the son of an Apache chief. On evenings when he'd changed into casual gear, it was always denims. In summer he'd wear T-shirts: sparkling white, terracotta, deep blue, but nothing too gaudy. Then she'd sneak a secret glance at his tanned skin and his lean protruding muscles. A sharp dart of desire would invariably score a hit in the pit of her stomach.

He never seemed to bother much with looks. Not once, in all the time she'd known him, had he actually told her she was attractive. When other men came up to her in bars and clubs and told her she looked pretty, he'd nod and say, "She's a very lovely lady, but there's much more to her than that!"

A few times a guy would persist and ask, "Are you a couple, or what?"

He'd answer, "She's my kid sister. I'm her chaperone!"

The only time he ever complimented her was when she wore long, Indian skirts or flowing, silk shirts.

"That really looks good!" He'd nod his head in approval. "That colour really suits you."

While they were friends he never once cast his eyes along her shapely legs, stole longing glances at her breasts, or stared, trance-like, at the curves of her body. She would have been acutely aware if he had. Strangers often stared like this when she walked into a room. It made her feel embarrassed, self-conscious and uneasy. But if he had looked at her like that it would have made a world of difference. She wanted to excite him. While he was living with another woman she would never have considered a sexual liaison. They were both too principled for that. But she was always searching for a sign, hanging on to his every word, hoping for some kind of tangible proof that she was special to him.

It surprised her that he had an old-fashioned respect for women. He was chivalrous. On a few occasions she witnessed him verbally castigating a guy for telling a lewd story that objectified women. He thought pornography was an illness.

"If a man can't get turned on by the real thing, if he needs kinky lingerie, sexy props or the like to arouse him, he has a serious problem. I've never been kinky in my life!"

He abhorred prostitution. Many a time in the freezing winter nights when he was living in a flat with Jean in Fitzwilliam Square, he'd ask a woman-of-the-night in for a cup of tea, or soup, or something stronger. He'd heard many of their stories: childhood abuse, alcoholism, drug-addiction, poverty, the promise of riches, the cold, dark nights, the risk and the dangers, the pimps, the sad and the bad and the ugly.

"Women who wear mini skirts," he told her one evening in The Stag's Head, "are demeaning themselves, falling in to the age-old trap that desirability is their most important attribute. It's different in summer. Then it's natural to want to feel cool and to let the sun warm your body. It's wearing mini skirts on freezing cold nights, with bare legs or wafer-thin tights, hobbling around in high-heels on a path of ice. All this to arouse the male's appetite! That's a definite form of masochism. I hate to see women being exploited by multi-million-dollar advertising industries, by cosmetic surgeons, by firms promoting magic slimming potions. Women are easy targets. Many have swallowed the advertiser's bait, hook, line and sinker: 'Unless you are counted a raving beauty, you are worthless, in a male world. You can only be a 'real' woman if you apply the right shade of lip gloss, wear the latest fashions, and eventually starve yourself until you no longer exist.' All this is a bunch of crap! It's deadly dangerous: a lethal form of mind control."

He was the first man she'd ever met who could put up a good case for being admitted to the feminist movement.

"You say men and women are treated equally in our society? Okay then. How many women do you know who retain their own names after marriage? Just think about it.

How many women are called Mrs.—the mistress of—after marrying? It's not only choice, it's the whole weight of tradition, of being acceptable socially. Anyway, what's marriage but a glorified form of prostitution?"

He paused to drink down the dregs of his Guinness.

"Women have for so long been brain-washed to believe that their only purpose in life is procreation and to please a man sexually. This was their lot, dictated by God and nature, or so they've been told for centuries, by lascivious, power-hungry males. That was often the extent of a woman's education. Imagine whole generations of women whose minds were never given the chance to stretch and breathe and blossom?"

For a man who upheld the sanctity of human intelligence, it was an unspeakable crime to keep billions of human beings ignorant of the unpolished jewel they possessed inside their heads. There was no doubt that Peter was different than any man she had ever met.

Within a few months there was an easy intimacy between them. In the long, summer evenings he'd often suggest a walk. He loved Dublin. It was his home. His childhood and teenage years had been spent in Malahide. When he met Jean they moved into their first flat in Thomas Street because they both wanted to live in the heart of the city. Since then they'd moved around many times, from Leeson Street to the South Circular Road, and from George's Street to Sandymount. Now they were settled in Clontarf. Jean drove a Cortina, so it wasn't much trouble for her to whiz from one side of the city to the other. Although he never said it, she felt Peter would prefer to live in the centre of things. He knew the streets, the pubs and the ancient buildings like the back of his hand. He had even spent a summer in his younger days, guiding tourists through the historical areas of the city. The pubs he knew from experience.

"Okay, m'lady, your guided tour starts here. To your right, Trinity College, built in 1592, under a charter of

Elisabeth the First. The library there is fantastic." He led her down side streets and tiny alleyways that she'd never even noticed before. For hours they'd walk, through old town gates and cobble-stoned paths. She could still see him standing there, taking a puff of his cigarette, while surveying the urban landscape.

"Across the road is another of my old haunts, The Castle Inn. That's where Jean and I used to go drinking when we lived in Thomas Street. That's part of my history. Okay, so now we reach a crossroads. We can keep going straight into The Liberties. It got its name because it was outside the Medieval City Walls and hence exempt from local jurisdiction. We could then pass through Thomas Street where Robert Emmet was hung, drawn and quartered. One of my ancestors, Sylvester, was arrested after the 1803 rising because he was suspected of being a supporter of Emmets'. In fact, he was a close friend. He was lucky to escape with his life. Rough times, m'lady. The next stop after Thomas Street could be Guinness' brewery in James Street. Or would you prefer to turn down into the heart of Viking Dublin: Winetavern Street, Wood Quay, St. Audoen's, Fishamble Street? The latter was the site of old fish shambles or markets in Viking times. It was also where Handel's *Messiah* was first performed in the old music hall at noon on April 13th, 1742. You don't mind? Well, m'lady, if you've no preference then I know where I want to go. Follow me!"

Peter dropped into The Brazen Head under the guise that it was part of their historic itinerary. It was the oldest pub in Dublin, frequented over the centuries by such eminent patrons as Wolfe Tone, Robert Emmett, and Daniel O'Connell. He had been in brilliant form that night, the life and soul of the pub. At the bar he met four Greeks. He brought them over to join their table.

"It's all this girl's fault. She's really worn me out tonight. No, not that! It was much more exciting than that. I escorted the lady on a tour of old Dublin. A pity you missed it. Viking Dublin, Medieval Dublin, Georgian Dublin. Would you like me to take you around some evening?"

The Greeks were ecstatic. Peter couldn't do enough for them. At any moment he would surely promise them the sun, moon and stars.

"Sure!" he beamed. "It's no problem. What about this Thursday? I could meet you here at, say, 6.30. Then we could walk maybe for two hours and resume our drinking here later. Maybe we'll do a circle of the city: James Street, Thomas Street, swerve around to Kevin's Street, then Stephen's Green, Kildare Street, Grafton Street, Dame Street, Wood Quay. Are you on for that too, Marion?"

Of course she was. Two nights in the same week! It sounded like heaven.

"That sounds good to me. I've nothing on this Thursday. Will I meet you here then?"

The truth was, that unless it was something of extraordinary importance, she would have cancelled it, without a moment's hesitation. It wasn't the same way for him, though. She had noticed a few times she'd rang, that he'd been quite cool, certainly not in good form. She had tentatively suggested an outing but he'd said something like, "Not tonight, Marion." He'd sounded tired and in no mood for persuasion. "I'm staying in for a change. I'm never at home. I need to catch up on that side of my life."

One Friday night they had arranged to meet and she had been as high as a kite, looking forward to it all week. That morning he'd phoned.

"I can't make it tonight, Marion. There's a pub quiz on at work and they insist I captain the team. It's the only way they'll have a God's chance in hell of winning. I'll ring you next week and we'll arrange something, okay?"

Back down to earth with a bang! Her kite had been stripped of its wings. Now it lay sapped, depleted. She never told him how disappointed she was. It was so different for him though, as when he was in good humour he could persuade her so easily to change her plans.

"You can go to that film anytime. You'll love this band. It's your choice but I've heard that film is crap. That's more like it. I thought your adventurous spirit had deserted you there for a minute."

There were definitely two extremes where his temperament was concerned. As sweet as honey or as sour and bitter as a lemon. Full of the joys of life and exuding charisma, or sullen, silent, dark and moody.

The music was good that night. She remembered the sound of tin whistles, a bodhrán, fiddles, a guitar, and uilleann pipes. Anyone could sing or join in if they liked. Peter had a lot to drink. The Greeks kept lining up the pints. They were so delighted with their congenial host. She knew he had a good voice. Many a time he'd sang a few bars of a tune to amuse her, but tonight he really excelled himself. The room went dead quiet. The musicians accompanied him. He sang one of her favourites, *Only our rivers run free.*

It was a beautiful rendition. His voice was deep, clear and full of feeling. He sang with eyes closed. The Greeks went berserk applauding.

"Bravo!"

"Splendid, my man!"

"Another Guinness for our friend, Peter, The Great!"

One of the women had tears in her eyes. She beckoned to Marion.

"Hold on to that man, my girl. He is so beautiful and charming. So sexy I'm sure! You are very blessed with him."

Marion felt a real sense of pride. He was her friend. But if only he was truly hers. The whole pub clapped, cheered and called for more. Was there no end to this man's talents?

She could still here his voice in her mind. She could still see his smile. The music had stopped, the colours were fading. Loneliness enveloped her like a rough, icy pall.

CHAPTER 6

It was cold standing at the fence but at least her back was against the breeze. A line of hedges made it difficult to view the mound properly. She looked around and then spotted a small elevated bank to her right, made of soil and stray tree-roots. This would surely give a clear view of the monument. It didn't take her long to clamber on top. She stood there motionless, her back against the bark of a huge stripped tree, partially shielding her from the cold, biting wind. It was a panoramic view: the white marble-like stones covered the entire facade, except for two dark, grey strips at either side of the entrance. The dark green of the surrounding countryside and the top of the mound provided a stark and wondrous contrast.

After standing there for a few minutes she badly needed to stretch her legs. She scrambled down the bank, then walked towards the entrance gate where the two Pre-Raphaelite girls were now standing, chatting with two of the Germanic men. The third of the tall, blonde brigade, who would have provided the main attraction at any Viking pageant, was taking a stroll himself.

"Hello!" he called to her. "Cold, isn't it?"

He must have been six feet three or four. His eyes were dark blue. He wore a woollen cap and gloves, a heavy jacket, black denims and thick walking boots.

"Yes. Especially when you're standing around waiting," she answered.

"Are you from this area?" he asked.

He stopped beside her, rubbing his hands and

stamping his feet, pulling his woollen cap further down over his ears. She was still trying to place his accent.

"I live in Dublin," she said. "It's not too far from here. But I'm originally from Wexford. Where are you from?"

Her curiosity got the better of her. She hoped he was from Norway or Finland. She'd love to visit these countries sometime, to see the spectacular fjords, the frozen lakes and the snow-covered trees.

"Myself and my friends are from Germany. I live in Hamburg. We've been travelling around Ireland for over three weeks. Before that we did some touring in Scotland. We still intend to head up north, to see Donegal and Antrim. I've heard the…how do you say it? The Giant's Causeway is quite spectacular. We stayed in Wexford for one day. The streets are so narrow there. It's a charming old town. We've already stayed one week in Dublin, and a couple of days in Galway, Kerry and Cork. The scenery there was amazing. I'm Christoff, by the way."

"Hello Christoff, I'm Marion."

There was no need for her to speak slowly or precisely. His English was virtually perfect. When he mentioned Hamburg she'd thought immediately of The Beatles who had gone there in the early '60s. Next to London, it must have been the rock capital of Europe then. She could visualise Peter standing next to her, quizzing this guy upside down about the music scene in Hamburg. But Peter wasn't standing beside her. This pleasant, uncomplicated German guy was.

"Is this your first time in Ireland?" she asked.

He shook his head. "No. I've been here three times before. Once during the summer when I was a student. I wanted to improve my English, but I preferred to visit Ireland much more than England. Then I returned with my girlfriend for a holiday three years ago. I came back again last year, on my own. I have become enchanted by the Irish culture, its beauty and its charm. So much of the land remains unspoilt. I love the beaches here and the fishing is good. The people too are really very friendly. Everyone is so relaxed. In Germany we spend most of our lives working and making money. In Ireland you really enjoy yourselves, with the Guinness, the *craic*, the pubs, and the music. It's a good life here. I love U2, Sinead O'Connor and The Cranberries. I've been to see The Dubliners and Christy Moore back home. Last week I went with some friends to hear The Chieftains in concert. We loved it. It was really brilliant."

His eyes shone and colour flowed back into his cheeks.

"But Hamburg is renowned for its music too." She figured he was too young to have been around in the height of the '60s, but he must be aware of his heritage. "All the big groups would have played there, even The Beatles. It must have quite a wild night-life, even still."

"Perhaps!" he shrugged his shoulders. "I suppose it's the same with everyone. You never appreciate what's on your own doorstep. There are some good places for music in Hamburg but I've become tired of life there. Whereas, with Ireland, it's a kind of love affair. It's just fantastic."

"So how come you've ended up in Newgrange at this early hour on a freezing cold morning?" she inquired.

"Ah!" he laughed. "I was fortunate enough last year to make some very good friends. They live in Drog-heda. So that is where we are staying at the moment. Our friend, Pat, told us about Newgrange and explained the Winter Solstice. The story really intrigued us so we came down to take a look for ourselves. Are you one of the fortunate ones who will be admitted inside?"

"Yes, indeed I am. I've waited many years for this morning. Now I'm just about forty minutes away. I'm so nervous though."

She visibly shivered as she thought about it–the immense privilege it was to be allowed entry to the chamber. It must have been ten years since her interest in Newgrange had been aroused. Her brother had bought her a book on ancient Irish sites. He knew she'd love the artwork. Newgrange had been featured. It was the first she'd ever heard of it. Now it had become woven into the very fabric of her life, with as thick and strong a thread as the man known as Peter Kerrigan.

"You must be very excited. I hope the sun will shine for you today."

He smiled. She hoped so too, that it would shine for the whole year ahead, bringing a balm to heal her wounds and restore her faith in life and love. She silently prayed that it would fill all their hearts with peace and light. In the background she noticed his friends beckoning. He spotted them too. Red-coated Nuala had also returned with pen and folder in hand.

"Excuse me, please. I will just see why my presence is required."

Marion walked back to the fence. More people continued to arrive in dribs and drabs. There must have been about forty now. No one had been admitted to the site yet. The sky had brightened considerably and there was very little cloud. Only that Red Nuala had informed her that sunrise wasn't due until almost nine, she would have been in a real tizzy. To miss the dawning of today's sun would be a personal catastrophe. But there was no need to worry. There was ample time left to indulge in further reverie...

Her friends had never liked him. Every month or so the gang would meet up in a pub, maybe go for a meal, to a film, or to some gig. A few times she'd invited him along. Most times he'd agreed to go but Jim hadn't liked him from the start.

"He's a know-all, Marion. He has to be right all the time. He's certainly challenging, but very critical. I'm sorry. I know you think the world of him. He treats you differently though than everyone else. He has a respect for you and your ideas. But the rest of us? He was downright rude and insulting the way he spoke to Conor. I don't think we're up to scratch for him somehow."

She had hoped Jim would like him. It had hurt that he hadn't. At least Niamh could understand why Marion was so attracted to Peter. He was certainly intelligent. He exuded both confidence and charisma. He had wild, dark bohemian looks, like a brooding Heathcliff. He had a wealth of personal experience of people and life. It was also clear that he had a definite soft spot for Marion.

It was easy to keep these two aspects of her life separate. For the first year or so she never saw Peter more than once a week. This meant there was loads of time for friends, for taking the odd night course in art, meditation and yoga, for connecting with family every few weekends, and for walking the Wexford beaches with her beloved nieces and nephews. Work also took up a lot of time. She had thought that research and compiling statistics on people's feelings and experiences would have been fascinating. The job didn't satisfy her though. Some part of her wanted to work at a much deeper level with people. She just wasn't sure yet what her particular slot in life would be. At twenty-four, with her psychology degree under her belt, she really wasn't too worried. There was plenty of time to make her mark on the world.

They each occupied a compartment of the other's life. His friends, his family and Jean remained in completely separate sections. There were a few friends that he met regularly. Some of them were also friends of Jean's. A couple of times Marion was with him in a pub when one of them appeared. She heard several of them whisper:

"Peter, are you still with Jean? What's the story?"

"Who's this then, Peter? Are you getting itchy feet? Things too settled? Need an extra bit of a twist?"

One of these guys, called Gerry, looked her upside

down, and inside out.

"She's gorgeous, Pete! A real dark-haired beauty. The split of Ali MacGarth. You haven't lost it then, mate."

Peter tried to laugh it off.

"She's another of my sisters, Gerry! Don't even try to figure it. We're friends."

Then there was the afternoon he'd rang her.

"Hi Marion. I've been up to my eyes all morning. The whole system has gone berserk. I haven't time to talk now. Just tell me one thing. Are you wearing your suit today?"

She laughed, delighted. This was one of his brilliant days. She always knew by the tone of his voice when he uttered his first sentence.

"Yes. I told you we'd have to dress up today for the project meeting. All the big bugs will be there."

She was wearing her one and only dark red suit and cream blouse. She felt way overdressed.

"Okay then. Are you on for meeting after work? Great! I'll meet you in HMV, Grafton Street. Does 5.45 suit? Brilliant. See you later. Toodle-oo!"

She knew he had something planned. Her heart was beating ninety to the dozen. This must have been the happiest time of her life.

"Hello there. Wow! A real yuppie! What is the world coming too when two of its leading dissenters are dressed like high-flying executives? Anyway, to save the day, I've just bought a really great album: Ry Cooder. Brilliant guitar. Okay. Now for our tour of yuppiedom!"

He led her down Grafton Street, then turned right into the Hibernian Mall. He pointed to a table.

"This is a good spot for observing the yuppie lifestyle. Coffee for you, madam? But of course; how remiss of me. It must be cappuccino for you and espresso for moi!" His voice had become yuppiefied. She couldn't stop laughing. He searched his jacket for his Silk Cut, then lit up and inhaled deeply.

"Do you have your filofax to arrange our next meeting?" His performance would surely earn him an Oscar. "And how is that portable CD player you bought in BTs? I hope you have your cell phone switched on, just in case someone rich and famous is trying to contact you? I hear they're all the rage in the US. Isn't it great to be part of the beautiful people, the elite, the nouveau-riche? Just a pity we don't have the designer hair styles to match our cool image." He broke into a grin. "That couple over there look as though they're just 'après ski'. I'm not exactly an expert in fashion but I have to say I'm gob-smacked. What a get up!"

She looked over at the young couple at the other side of the café. The girl wore a neon-coloured ski suit while her cohort sported a dark orange shirt that was tucked into navy, parachute pants.

"I know! Keep your mouth shut, Kerrigan. When it comes to fashion you haven't a clue!"

Marion pretended she was choking on a biscuit as she struggled to smother her laughter.

"I knew you'd enjoy this palaver!" He couldn't stop laughing too.

Of course she loved every minute. It made no difference where they were or what they were doing. Life oozed excitement and joy whenever he was in that sparkling mood, radiating that special glow.

"The brother, Ken, the banker, there's a real yuppie if ever you saw one. The Ma is always wracking her brain, wondering where she went wrong. He was always an oddball, though, a right pain in the hole. His wife is even worse. A real right-wing bible-basher. We've nearly come to fists the last few times we've banged into each other. I know: live and let live and all that, but he really gets under my wick."

He drank down the last of his espresso and then pulled his jacket from the back of the chair.

"Are you ready? Time to push on. Follow me, madam."

Back onto Grafton Street, then right into the Westbury Hotel. She had heard this was the most expensive in Dublin.

"Another coffee? I think dinner is out of the question. I forgot my string of credit cards. We'll just make a quick stop here. Now you see why I asked if you were suitably attired? When you're hanging out with Kerrigan you've got to have style. I've a standard to keep up, you know!"

Half an hour later they were back on Grafton Street.

"Now for my favourite yuppie spot."

He walked towards Stephen's Green, Marion close in pursuit. He took a left.

"The Shelbourne is next, madam. It's Victorian. Notice the pair of Nubian princesses and their slave girls at the entrance. The ones with the fettered ankles are the slaves. When The Rolling Stones come to town they take over an entire floor here. More pseudo-hippies showing their true colours. Sad isn't it?"

This time he led her to the bar. It was a spectacular building, exquisitely decorated with crystal chandeliers and full-length portraits.

"An aperitif, Marion?"

While he was at the bar she sized up the clientele. Most of the guys wore dark suits while the girls were dressed in skirts and jackets of various hues, complete with the obligatory shoulder pads.

He placed their drinks on the table, then followed her gaze.

"It's kind of like being extras in Dynasty!" he smirked. "At least I'm glad there's none of that canned music to distract us. You have to be careful these days or your ears could be assailed by the most brutal racket imaginable."

He sank into his Guinness.

real meaning in their lives. Money and expensive toys are the new Gods. People actually believe that these things will bring happiness, kill the pain and fill the void. But I know there's a dimension to all people that yearns for a deeper meaning in life, to fulfil our creative potential. I call this dimension spiritual."

"I agree with the sentiment," he nodded. "Forget 'spiritual' though. The human dimension will do me. Sometimes the pain is so great you'd do anything to quash it. But not everyone has the skills, the support or the will to change their lot, Marion. Now, before I get too involved here, it's time for reinforcements. What's it this time? A potent cocktail or a mind-blowing Ballygowan?"

She pushed her hands deep inside her pockets. The truth was that she'd give almost anything to relive just one of those nights. It had all seemed so natural and low-key at the time. She had felt so secure in their friendship. So certain of his affection. She had trusted him completely. There were so many snap-shots, instances frozen in time that flitted across her mind, frame after frame. The reel came to a screeching halt. One of those moments now breathed new life...

It was the evening he'd produced the photos. He had taken them while holidaying in Greece. They'd gone for a meal that evening. They were both ravenous after skipping lunch. Peter relished his glass of white wine then lit up his customary cigarette. Soft music played in the background. The waiter lit the red candle at the centre of the table, presuming they were young lovers. If only! The food was delicious. Peter was starry-eyed. The whole atmosphere was so romantic. The conversation had taken many turns and had now arrived at the Pantheon, in Athens. He had taken a wonderful shot of the old, white ruins in very soft, early morning light. The next was of the famous Minoan caves in Crete. Then all of a sudden, like a flaming thunderbolt out of the blue, Marion came face to face with Jean.

Her heart sank. It was one thing to know that most of Peter's life was shared with a woman named Jean, but having him produce a photograph was undisputable evidence. Imagine how she'd feel if she actually saw them together? She struggled to catch her breath. She felt as if she was choking. In an instant the room felt stark and chill.

Of course, he'd often mentioned Jean. Marion had so far gathered she'd trained as an artist before working as an interior designer. Her family must have been quite rich because they had loaned her the deposit for their home in Clontarf. There had been a time when they'd spent all their evenings together. Almost all of their friends had been mutual. All-night parties, pubs, clubs, and live music sessions had then been the norm. He had never pretended. They had been very much in love.

"Intimacy changes things."

He held the precious photo carefully at the edges.

"When you live with someone and share your space and your life, it's not easy. You have to be very creative to keep on finding new things to keep each other amused, new ways of showing the other person you still really care. All your strengths and weaknesses become exposed. There's no hiding place. There are moments when you can reach the heights of rapture, and then with one word, one look, you can be banished to hell. The agony and the ecstasy. The cycle of pleasure closely followed by pain. The anger and the hurt. Alas, I figure that's the natural progression of love and life."

He was still staring at the photo that he held carefully, almost reverently, between his fingers.

"I've never loved anyone the way I loved Jean."

He glanced up at Marion.

"Maybe it's better though when two people in a relationship begin to experience new aspects of life. That keeps the fires alive."

He reached for his glass and sipped his white wine.

"Jean was so magnetic, so drop-dead gorgeous when I met her," he continued. "I liked her hair that way: layered, kind of wild. She cut it a few years ago. It's nearly shorter than mine now. That makes her look much harder. This photo is the best one I ever took of her."

He handed her a picture of a woman lying on a rock that jutted far out into the sea. The sky and the water were turquoise. The woman aged in her mid-twenties. She was wearing a loose, see-through robe over a cerise bikini. Her hair was long and blonde, glistening in the sunlight. Her skin was tanned and well oiled, her body perfect in every detail. Her face reminded Marion of someone. That was it! Michelle Pfeiffer. Her eyes were blue, reflecting the colour of the sea. She was certainly beautiful.

Jealousy and pain. She couldn't deny the emotions. The reality was that Peter lived with this woman and loved her. Marion knew she was just his friend.

"She's very pretty," she said.

She had to speak the truth; anything else would have exposed her deflated mood.

"And it certainly looks like a paradise island."

She had to change the subject. She could never show him for an instant how much he meant to her. To be that vulnerable would cripple her, and anyway, what would be the point? His relationship had hit a rough patch–that was obvious. That's why he'd wanted a new friend. He liked being with her. She was innocent and posed no sexual threat. If it was sex he was looking for he would never have chosen her. He had already told her that two of his female acquaintances had recently made advances. He'd replied by stating the facts: he was not a dishonest man. He was living with Jean and was sexually involved, only with Jean.

The frustration, the pain and the inner confusion of

that night flooded her mind. That was about three years ago. Memory can produce such an exact replica of a time and a place long since passed. What was time? In one's imagination you could relive any moment. Days, weeks, months, years, decades: all can be pondered and scanned in the twinkling of an eye.

She brought her attention to the present once again. Newgrange. This was a timeless place, a sanctuary, where a tired soul could curl up in the depths of its strong, comforting arms. Who knows but that it had always existed, in the deep recesses of the human psyche?

CHAPTER 7

She glanced at her watch. It had been a gift for her twenty-first from her parents: gold strap and black face with Roman numerals. It was 8.20. Time was passing slowly but she didn't mind. Jim and Niamh would probably have come with her, even if they had to remain outside. But she had wanted to be here alone, to have space to think, to remember...

He had never given a gift of jewellery in his life.
"I'm not one for buying presents. I do like to give the special people in my life the odd gift from time to time."
They were sitting in O'Donoghue's. It was a dark, grey evening, about a week before Christmas. A little lamp was lighting in the back room.
"This reminds me of a Rembrandt." He surveyed the scene with his dark, luminous eyes. "Everything is in shadow, except for the tiny flicker of light in the corner. Rembrandt's palette was always fairly scant: burnt umber, yellow ochre, cadmium red, with a touch of lemon yellow. No one can beat the Dutch for painting interiors. They were masters of chiaroscuro—using strong contrasts between light and dark. Anyway, it's the perfect scene for a quiet December drink."
She had taken a half-day from work to do her Christmas shopping. There was pandemonium in the stores. Crowds jostled and pushed to grab their obligatory gifts. It had taken over three hours to unearth some classy items. She'd bought her mother a chic blouse. For her

favourite aunt she'd chosen a silk scarf, and for her niece, Sarah–Greg's daughter–she'd bought the golden angel she'd been raving about. The remainder she'd tackle on Saturday.

She had wanted to give Peter a gift but she had no idea what to choose. She knew his lack of sentimentality: Not the kind of man you'd give a few pairs of socks to. She decided the best thing was to write him a short story, about life and love, dreams and beliefs, feelings and soul connections. *Kindred Spirits* she'd called it. She planned to give it to him just before they parted. She wouldn't see him then for over three weeks.

"I like to buy my friends' kids something unusual."

Another sip of Guinness. He was settling down for a long night.

"I've known Joe and Marie for aeons. I first met Joe when we compared pub quizzes in McDaid's. They have two fantastic kids. Leone is about four and Karina is just six. I love those kids. They have a lot more intelligence than most adults I know. This year I spotted a brilliant game called *Moviemaker*. I'm sure they'll get a lot of fun out of it and it's pretty educational too."

He lit up a Silk Cut and inhaled, then breathed out a stream of smoke.

"When I'm buying for adults then it'll probably be a tape or a book", he continued. "On very rare occasions it'll be something personal, something I've created myself. I always give my sister a book for Christmas. I ask her first what period of history she's currently studying. Last year it was Egypt. This year it's megalithic monuments."

He reached for his pint and drank down a few mouthfuls. Then he resumed his monologue.

"I saw a brilliant book yesterday that covers megalithic communal burial chambers dotted around Europe. I read the first few pages. The cutting of the huge stones and the similarity of construction over such a wide area indicates a homogenous pre-Celtic culture. That's kind of fascinating! You've mentioned an interest in Newgrange before. Lisa, the sister, is into all that at the moment. Yeah, I think that's the best gift for her."

Another similarity, Marion thought. The book her brother, Greg, had bought for her eighteenth birthday had first introduced her to the magical world of Newgrange. Now Peter was buying his sister a book on megalithic monuments, the greatest of all these sites being Newgrange. But whatever about his sister, Marion couldn't help wondering what he had chosen for Jean. Of course she was curious, but simultaneously she prayed he wouldn't even mention it.

"That book sounds great," she said. "It's a present I'd be delighted with. I've been to Newgrange several times. It's a wonderful place: a time-machine to transport one through the ages. Another three years to go and then I'll get the chance to be in the chamber on the morning of the solstice."

It seemed so far away then. Now it was but minutes away.

"Yeah? Well you're a very lucky lady. That will be an amazing experience, for sure. Newgrange is a passage grave, isn't it? A dolmen with a long stone roofed entrance passage, constructed on several upright supports and a flat roofing slab, all covered with a protective mound of earth. Do you know the exact meaning of megalithic? Huge, undressed stones used in various types of Neolithic and early bronze-age monuments. Neolithic refers to the last ten thousand years of earth history. I read all about it yesterday in the bookshop."

That deserved another swig. He licked his lips.

"Not bad after glancing at a few pages in the heat of the Christmas rush," he laughed.

She shook her head. His memory was phenomenal. She wished she had his ease of retention.

"It's the gargle," he smirked. "Enough of ancient

monuments. Let's get into the Christmas spirit, whatever that is. I have a proposition. I've taped you a selection of the best music of all time. Now, we can't go back to my place because Jean is entertaining. So how about your place? As long as you have a good tape deck!"

Her stomach turned inside out and upside down.

"Sure!"

She tried to sound cool. He must have noticed her sudden flush of emotion.

"You'll be quite safe. I'm the nearest thing to a married man, remember? Anyway, if I'm ever thinking of making a pass at you I promise to ask you first, okay? But tonight I have a better idea. When we get to your flat I'd like to sketch you, if you're on for it. I have some paper and pencils with me. All you'll have to do is pose—fully clothed I mean—unless you insist on going au naturel! It won't take more than ten minutes. I'd really like to draw you though."

They walked through bustling crowded streets. It was late night shopping in the city. The streets were alive with buskers and carol singers; street traders plying their wares; trees and fairy lights; dazzling shop windows; department stores bursting with panicked shoppers; wide-eyed children pointing in wonder; elegant party-goers in velvet, lace and furs. Then there were the young cooing couples, dressed to the hilt, walking arm in arm, breathless with laughter.

Peter steered her down a side street.

"This is madness," he laughed. "And there's worse to come. I advise you to get out of Dublin well before Christmas Eve. I might clear out myself yet. The Aran Islands would be nice at this time of year."

Marion smiled up at him. Part of her felt elated, buoyant. She was walking beside Peter and nothing else really mattered. But there was another side that secretly pondered the wisdom of giving her soul to a man who was living with another woman. If she continued this friendship there would never be room for another love to enter her life. Perhaps she would never know what it felt like to be held, to be loved. He probably wondered himself why she wasn't romantically involved with anyone. A few times he'd asked subtle questions about Jim, Anto and Conor. He'd wondered what kind of relationship she had with them. She had told him the truth.

"Taxi!" he called.

He was always generous. As far as she could see he spent vast fortunes on drink, dining out, music, books and transport.

"Rathmines," he instructed the driver, "if you can manoeuvre your way through that traffic!"

They stopped for a take-away along the route. She said she wasn't hungry but he bought enough to feed an army.

"You'll need to keep your strength up. This could be a long night."

She lived alone. She liked it that way. In college she'd stayed with Niamh and Sharon. When she started work she moved in with Lynn for a while. She had even stayed with Jim for a few months. She had enjoyed those times immensely. It had been a new venture to move out on her own but there was rarely a shortage of company. Almost any weekend she stayed in Dublin one of the gang would sleep on her sofabed. But she liked to be in control of her space. It wasn't a palace. Compared to his home, decorated no doubt by his interior-designer girlfriend, it must have seemed fairly tacky. Most of her paintings and sculptures she kept in her family home in Curracloe. Rathmines was a phase of life she was simply passing through. Someday she'd have her own place and then it would be really classy.

She'd bought three bookcases to house the hundreds of books she'd accumulated over the years. He flicked through a few of the titles. A couple of colourful tapestries hung on the walls. Her white, cuddly dog sat on an armchair, a present from Jim. He placed it on his knee.

"Say hello to Marion, the mistress of the manor."

Surely ventriloquism wasn't another of his talents! He rarely showed this little-boy side of himself. He really made her laugh.

When the pizza had been consumed and the coffee pot lay brewing on the table he took out his pencils and pad. He waved her to the sofa.

"Now lie back there, Marion, and try to get comfortable. I'll just turn out this overhead light and switch on the lamp instead. That's perfect. Now, just tilt your head a little to the right. I need your face to be centre of the light. That's it. I'm no Rembrandt or Vermeer but I've sketched for as long as I can remember. Are you relaxed there? Great! Don't worry, it won't take too long."

She tried to relax but her heart kept pounding. This felt too intimate for comfort. He was staring at her, taking in every detail of her face. Running his eyes along her neck and breasts. She was all too aware of what she was wearing, a slinky, pure wool jumper which left little to the imagination. She hoped he liked what he saw.

"What about a smile for the artist? Enjoy the experience! I've sketched quite a few friends before. I did one of Leone and Karina–the two kids I was telling you about. I was really happy with the way it turned out. I've drawn Lisa, the sister, a couple of times. And I've done a few sketches of Jean. She was impressed and I can assure you she's not an easy woman to please!"

She blushed as the question formed in her mind: Had Jean been naked when he'd sketched her?

"Not long now. I don't like to make a song and dance about art. So many so-called experts take years to get any kind of likeness. Just finishing off the shading. Yeah, that's captured the lady pretty well, I think. Happy Christmas, Marion."

He reached across the coffee table and placed the

•

sketch in her hands.

She was startled by the familiarity of the face that stared up at her. Yes, it was an excellent likeness. If anything, she looked a little too pretty. He'd captured her smile, her eyes, her hair, and yes–even her breasts–all to perfection. She was thrilled.

"Thanks a million, Peter. It's really a great likeness. It's amazing what you can do with a few pencils. I have the perfect frame I can put it in. I'm really delighted with it."

She was still a little embarrassed. He shrugged his shoulders.

"It's your inspiration, Marion! Now, for recreation. Lead me to the music system."

She pointed to the far corner of the room. The stereo had cost her over a month's salary but she'd felt it was well worth it. The sound was superb. Many an evening when she was there alone she'd put on some of her favourite rock tunes and dance herself crazy.

"Now let the music roll! How high can I turn this knob? Are the neighbours big into rock and blues? I sure hope so!"

He handed her the hand-written cover that listed the songs he'd taped. They were all her favourites. The songs played long into the night, scanning the decades, setting her alight with wild guitars and deep soul vibrations. He pulled off his shoes, lowered himself onto the floor and lay there, sometimes singing, sometimes sleeping.

She remembered falling asleep. Sometime during the night she awoke to find herself covered up on the sofa. Peter was spread out across an armchair. He opened his eyes and smiled.

"I suppose I'd better be going. I need to be home before dawn. It's a kind of unwritten rule. It doesn't matter where you go or what you do, just as long as you both end up under the same roof before sun-up."

He sat up slowly, then pulled on his shoes.

She nodded. She didn't want him to go but he was going anyway. She suddenly remembered her gift for him. She reached for her bag and pulled out an envelope.

"This is for you. Just something I wrote; a kind of short story."

He took it and put it under his arm.

"Thanks. I'll read it over the weekend. We won't get a chance to meet now until after Christmas. I'll give you a call next week before the holidays. I enjoyed the music. See you, Marion."

He waved, opened the door and was gone.

She carried the precious sketch into her bedroom. It was a souvenir she would always treasure. She turned off the light, crawled into bed and fell into a deep sleep...

She glanced up to see Nuala standing at the gate again, welcoming several more newcomers. The sky was definitely brightening with each minute that passed. Casting her eyes to the east she willed the dark clouds that covered the sun's lair to disperse. Still, there was time enough for the clouds to fade and the heralding of a spectacular dawn. She strolled along by the fence, setting her mind free once again to recreate another scene...

That was reminiscent of so many nights. Sometimes he'd race out the door at six in the morning. But he always returned to Jean. And during all that time he had never once touched her.

He rang the following Monday, all delighted with her story.

"I was really impressed. You've a good way with words and you're very observant when it comes to detail. I was surprised though that it was a bit erotic in places. Surprised, but thrilled! We can all do with an extra portion of spice to liven up our mundane lives."

"I'm glad you liked it," she choked. She had taken a risk in showing him some of her feelings under the guise of the leading lady. But it had been worth it.

"If you like, we can write each other poems and stories. I like dabbling around with words, as you know. It'd be good fun."

"I'd love to!" She nearly dropped the receiver she was so ecstatic.

"Great. So we'll have some good fun in the New Year. You say you're heading home tomorrow. I've nothing much planned. It'll be a very quiet Christmas. I may even do a bit of overtime on Stephen's day. Anyway, I'd better go here. Things are hotting up. Have a good Christmas and let me know when you're back in town. Bye!"

She cupped her hands over her mouth and blew hard. She was beginning to feel the wintry frost melting into her limbs. She replaced her gloves and paced along the fence. The wheels turned again inside her head and the memories poured forth, with crystal clarity...

It was April. They had known each other a whole year and eight months. She had looked it up on the calendar. It was her twenty-fifth birthday.

"It's next Thursday. I'd like to do something to mark the day. I'm just arranging with a few friends to go to a gig. I'm not sure where. Of course you're invited. Any ideas? And how was your trip by the way?"

It used to be a weekly phonecall but over the last month he'd begun to call more often. Two weeks ago he'd sounded in desperate form. They had met in The Palace Bar. He said he'd had a row with Jean. She'd threatened to throw him out. Marion tried to keep out of it. It was hard to be a sympathetic listener when she felt so deeply involved. She knew he was hurting but she didn't know what to do. She told him if he ever needed a place to stay he could kip out with her.

"It's like trying to cling onto a cliff-edge while a gale-force wind belts your face and the icy rain cuts your fingers to the bone. I'm afraid I'm falling into an abyss."

He had planned a week away with Jean in the South of France.

"To rekindle the spark", he'd said.

They had spent their first holiday in Saint-Tropez. Peter must have believed that returning there would somehow bring back the love they had obviously once shared. At the last minute Jean had refused to go. He went alone. Marion felt confused. She hated to see him so down, but she would have felt very jealous if he'd gone away with Jean. It was a crazy situation.

"You sound much better, that's for sure."

She was delighted to hear the old Peter again.

"I feel better this week. France was warm and sunny. I met plenty of friendly locals. In the evenings the music and the beer were great. I spent most days on the beach. It was quite deserted so I just read, drank, sketched, and soaked up the sun. Things are better with Jean now. We had a good talk at the weekend. We've made it up again. The trials and tribulations of life!"

She closed her eyes and shook her head. He was still with Jean.

"So you'll be twenty-five this week! A mere child. It's not far off 'till my thirtieth. I figured a long time ago that age is all in the head. Sometimes I feel more like fifty. And as for you, you're more like twenty. And I mean that in a good way. You've no responsibilities, no ties. You're free and unfettered."

He paused, seemingly waiting for a reaction.

"Sure!" she smiled as she glanced at the hundreds of questionnaires piled up on the desk waiting for her to sort and analyse. "I don't feel very free here at the moment, but I'll take your word for it!"

"Well, you mentioned next Thursday. The brother is playing in McGonigal's that night. Jean will be there too. I've told her all about you. She said she'd like to meet you. I was going to suggest you could come over for dinner some evening at the house, maybe watch a video or something. But it'd probably be better to meet up at a gig. Your friends could come too, if you'd like."

More confusion. The thought of Jean knowing anything about her made her queasy. She could imagine him saying, 'I've got this really interesting friend. Marion's her name. She's really intelligent, a very cultured girl. I'm sure you'd like her. I think you'll have a lot in common.' The only thing they had in common was Peter as far as she was concerned.

"I'll think about it," she said.

She wasn't sure if it was a good idea. What would Jim think of this set-up? And her work buddy, Lynn? They would surely think she was cracked. Meeting Jean held a terrible fear for her. Perhaps facing it would help her dispel the myth of the beautiful, exquisite female who occupied pole position in Peter's life. She could arrive well armed, surrounded by her legion of friends as protectors.

"I'll mention it to the gang," she replied. "I'll call you on Wednesday to let you know if it suits."

She had been to McGonigal's before. It was noted for giving new bands a break into the music scene. Her friend, Anto, had once brought her along to hear his girlfriend sing with a heavy metal band called The Creeps. She had arranged to meet Peter after work. Lynn and Niamh would meet them at the gig. Jean was due to turn up around nine. Marion had butterflies in her stomach. She had changed into a new, black skirt and a gold, silk top. If she ever needed to look good it was tonight. Then again, a make-over from top to toe wouldn't have gone amiss, seeing she was meeting the blonde, blue-eyed beauty. She had looked in the mirror to reassure herself before leaving work. Her skin was smooth and glowing, her hair was gleaming and the gold-coloured top fitted her like a glove.

"To hell with them all," she tried to boost herself up. "I'm going to enjoy myself tonight!"

At least she was meeting Peter on his own first. That should give her time to compose herself.

"Hi! Happy birthday and all that. First things first, drink?"

He certainly looked bronzed and well rested. He wore a soft, creamy shirt with a few buttons at the top left undone. She couldn't help glancing at the tight chest muscles whenever he stretched across the table to take up his pint. He was simply stunning.

He admired her attire. That was a promising start. He had written a story for her while lying on the golden sands on the Riviera. She was thrilled. She wanted to read it there and then but he asked her to keep it until later. She placed the envelope carefully in her bag.

Looking at him sitting opposite she wondered if he was nervous, or what exactly he was feeling. He seemed quite calm, nothing unusual. She told him about her weekend trip to Galway. She had gone with Niamh, Conor and Jim, and they'd stayed with their college friend, Orla, and her husband. They'd driven to Connemara on the Saturday. It was her first time there and she raved about it. That night they'd found a tiny pub with the best blues sound of all time. He said he'd often been to Galway. It had been a favourite haunt of Jean and his in the early days. All roads invariably led back to Jean.

They arrived at McGonigal's just a little before nine. Lynn and Niamh were already there. Peter disappeared for a while to have a word with his brother. Niamh was making a big effort to keep Marion in good spirits. She knew the story intimately. She hadn't liked the idea of Marion spending her birthday walking a tight rope between Peter and his woman. The background music had a good beat. A few people were already dancing.

"Will we shake a leg?" Niamh asked.

They were just getting up from the table when Peter appeared. There was a woman trailing behind him.

"Jean, this is Niamh, Lynn, and Marion."

She would never have recognised her in a thousand years. Jean had certainly changed. Her hair was cropped short. Her eyes looked lifeless, tired. She seemed ill at ease. She was still attractive but a drastic transformation had somehow occurred. She wore a white shirt, grey trousers and a long trench coat. She was nothing like the beauty in the photo, the glamourous woman who lay on the rocks, blissfully sunbathing in Greece.

Peter glanced at Marion. "I'm sure you'll have a lot to discuss—music and all. Jean is a big fan of Neil Young."

"Yes! I've been to three of his concerts. I love his Decade album." She tried to keep her voice from shaking.

"That's good." Jean answered curtly.

Peter jumped to the rescue. "Marion is big into Newgrange."

He was obviously struggling to find some common ground. He turned to Jean.

"You've always been into sacred sites yourself, though I've already spelled it out to Marion that our interest is purely archaeological, and not to the zillionth degree spiritual."

Jean shrugged her shoulders. "We're anything but spiritual," she answered coldly.

"We've had some fierce nights discussing the whole God-thing, haven't we?" Peter smiled at Marion.

"Yes, we certainly have."

The last time she'd felt this awkward was at her uncle's funeral, when searching for some words of comfort for her favourite aunt. But at least Peter was including her.

"I told you I'd introduced Marion to the pub-crawling life. That's where the best debates always take place. And in return she's given me a few psychological tips to help straighten me out. But as you know, nothing has worked yet." He looked over at Jean again.

"Is that all she's given you?" Jean snapped.

It was unnerving the way she stood there, staring ahead, never once making eye contact. Her face was expressionless, her body rigid, yet Marion could feel the rising tide of seething fury gathering inside her.

"It's always great fun being with Peter. I never quite know what he's going to do next?" Marion retaliated.

"I bet he's a bundle of laughs. I'm going to the bar."

Jean turned her back and walked away abruptly. When she'd gone Peter smiled weakly.

"She's just annoyed with me. Don't ask me what it's about, but it's nothing to do with you. I'll see if I can talk her 'round. Would you like a drink?"

"No. I'm fine." Marion shook her head.

"Right. Then I'll be back over later."

He turned and followed in the footsteps of Jean.

At that moment a familiar sound bashed the airwaves. The opening bars of *Freebird.*

"Come on!" Niamh shouted. "Let's go wild."

And they did. The tension of the night exploded through Marion's body. She turned and twisted, glided and freaked as the guitar strings wrapped themselves around her spinning spinal cord. She guessed Peter was watching from somewhere in the darkness. And what of Jean? The music drowned out all reason. It was like a serum, tuning out all pain, turning on waves of ecstasy. Niamh's red hair sprayed out before her as she rocked and swayed. Lynn's yellow, curly mane took on a life of its own. They danced in a circle: the three Goddesses, hugging and teasing. She could feel the music pulse through her veins. She went crazy.

"Now a big welcome for The Asylum!"

There was no mistaking the tall, dark figure in front. A carbon copy of the original. Peter came up to join them, pint in hand. Jean must be still part of the darkness.

"Can you guess which one is Kerrigan?" he laughed.

"It's not very difficult!" Marion pointed.

He nodded. "He thinks he's Morrison. He's even got the leather trousers. Not a bad voice though."

He was quite attractive too. Long, dark hair, skin-tight leathers and a deep growling voice. He did a few Doors' cover versions: *People are strange, Soul kitchen,* and the great pinnacle of the night, *Light my fire.* The floor was soon thronged. They retreated to their table. Still no sign of Jean. Peter disappeared again. The Asylum performed their final number. A few minutes after the gig ended they saw Jean emerging from the crowd, with Peter in close pursuit. She was heading for the exit.

"I've got to run. If I don't leave now I won't get a lift. I'll be in touch. Happy birthday Marion."

Then he was swallowed by the crowd.

"She has you on a string!" Marion thought to herself. "But even that won't ruin my birthday."

It was long past midnight before she had a chance to open the brown envelope he'd given her. It was the story of a man and a woman, both desperately in love. She read on, intrigued.

...The man was proud and independent, the woman soft and yielding. He took her for granted. He flaunted his arrogance and his self-belief. There were layers of his mind no one could reach, but she kept on striving, seeking, searching. He thought it was enough to love with part of his heart, and to keep the remainder concealed. She tired from her efforts and from his lack of response. She turned her sights to greener fields, where fertile pastures lay wide-open, unfettered. When he realised what was happening he felt panic and shock. The thought of losing her jolted him, aroused him from his apathy. He was now prepared to bear his all. But she had built a wall of stone around her. He had been so wrapped

up in his own world that he hadn't even noticed the blocks being raised, one by one, over months and years. Now it was complete.

For days he tried to breach the walls, then lay down, exhausted. For weeks he tried to find the key, but all attempts failed. He was on the verge of despair when he chanced to meet a friend. Fresh and alive like the wind and the sea. He was old and beaten, but she breathed new light into his eyes. And there were times when he actually laughed again. She had walls too, but hers were made of glass. He had glimpsed her inner world. He knew her better than she knew herself. He would have loved to ease her glass door gently open, to give her his hand, to help her step through. Yet he was chained to a stonewall, living in hope of salvation, committed to keeping a vigil lest his chance of redemption dawned. It was seldom his love came to him now. She had hardened like her stone surround. He felt very much alone. Even if it was the death of him he could never walk away.

CHAPTER 8

It was three weeks before they met again. She had called several times but he sounded dark and unreachable.

"I've got a lot of sorting out to do, Marion. I need some space. Not from you in particular, but just time to figure things out alone. I'll meet you soon. I could do with some of your professional skills. But I'll explain everything when we meet."

She stamped her feet and wrung her arms to keep warm. She remembered it had been a cold rainy evening when they'd finally met. She had sat in The Stag's Head waiting for him, wondering what had been happening in his life. Had he finished with Jean? After the way he'd been treated at McGonigal's she wouldn't be at all surprised. She could sense that something major had happened. She couldn't sit still, nor quieten the swarm of butterflies that fluttered inside her stomach.

"Hello stranger!" He looked really pleased to see her but his eyes looked tired and haggard. "Let me get you a drink. The usual?"

Too much drink and not enough sleep, she'd thought. At this rate he'd burn himself out like Hendrix and Morrison. But she was truly delighted to be with him again. She'd really missed him.

He sat down opposite, placing the customary pint of Guinness in front of him. He lit up a cigarette, inhaled deeply, then exhaled a long trail of smoke.

"I've had a really rough few weeks," he began.

"That's why I look so wretched. I'm sure you've noticed the black circles!"

He took a long sip then leaned back in his seat.

"It was the Saturday night after your birthday. On this rare occasion both of us stayed in. We had a blazing row. We've had some rough arguments before but this was different. It was vicious. They say that when lovers fight they really know how to attack with venom. Anyway, Jean said we were finished, that it was *kaputt*, over. She told me to leave. So I packed a bag and spent the night in a B&B. It's embarrassing even to think about it. I've hardly told anyone. But since you're about the only friend I have, I needed to tell you."

He paused to drink more of his Guinness.

"Ah! I needed that. Anyway, since then I've stayed with a guy from work. He's separated so he has a fair idea of the turmoil I'm going through."

"That's desperate, Peter." She was speechless.

"It's a crazy set-up, I know, to be virtually locked out of your own home. The things we do for love!"

He shrugged his shoulders and tried to laugh it off but she could see the deep hurt in his eyes.

"These last three weeks I've spent most evenings walking around Dublin like a zombie, wracking my brain, searching for a solution. There were lots of times I thought of you and really wanted to meet you, but I knew I had to get this mess sorted out in my head first."

He paused for another drink.

"It sounds like a nightmare, " she said. "But you could have stayed with me. I've a spare bed, remember?"

She struggled to sound calm herself. She wondered what was coming next. Had he finally split with Jean? Is that what he wanted to tell her? Her heart began pounding, but he was speaking again.

"Yeah, sure. But that wouldn't have sounded too good to the 'trouble-and-strife'! I was still determined to find some common ground between us. If you'd only known us in the early days. We were inseparable."

He stubbed out his cigarette then took another drink. The colour was returning to his cheeks.

"I arranged to meet her on Thursday evening," he continued, "to see if we could patch things up. It was weird, meeting like strangers in a coffee shop after all we've been through. We're probably in need of some kind of counselling but neither of us is into that. We feel bad enough without having to air our intimate details to a complete stranger. Anyway, we've admitted that things have been going downhill fast for the last few years. I suppose we just let them drift. We pretty much lived separate lives. It's not a question of who's to blame. I mean, believe it or not, I'm not exactly easy to live with! Well, to get to the nub of the tale, last weekend she agreed to take me back. I moved in on Saturday. We sorted out a lot of crap that evening over a Chinese and a few bottles of wine. So everything is rosy again. We're back in love. Quite a melodrama, isn't it?"

Marion could feel her face burning and her heart sinking. The disappointment was total. She didn't really want to hear any more. He was still with Jean. That was the bottom line. Even though she'd treated him like dirt, even forcing him out of his own home–practically in the middle of the night– he still loved her. She felt sick inside.

"It must have been difficult to go back, after all that's happened." She felt she had to say something.

"It was." He looked directly into her eyes. "But you must know how it is, not only professionally, I mean. I'm sure you've felt that way before about someone. Maybe you've never lived with a guy but the thought of admitting failure and of giving up the battle is hard to do. Wasn't there a guy in college you were with? Remember what those feelings were like when it was about to end? It kind of sucks you back in and you keep hanging on by your fingernails, even when it's probably destroying you."

Looking at him sitting there, lighting up another

cigarette, drinking down his pint, she wondered if he had any idea what she felt for him. Yes, love could probably destroy you.

"Yes, I was with John for a while. It was painful when we split, but I recovered."

"And what about now?"

She knew what was coming. He'd never asked her before. She felt embarrassed, extremely uncomfortable. He lowered his voice. He was watching her intensely.

"Is there another John in your life?" he asked.

"Not at the moment." She struggled to keep her cool. "I've a lot of male friends as you know, but that's as far as it goes."

She took a few sips of water to cool her throbbing head. He mustn't have a clue what she felt for him.

"Well, you're probably better off. Freedom is a rare gift. Anyway, that's my harrowing tale. Now tell me, what have you been up to?"

She was glad of a chance to camouflage her feelings, with talk of Niamh, work, and the Bon Jovi concert she'd gone to. It was becoming quite a strain to keep pretending. She just wanted to melt away, to dissolve, to escape the pain. He still loved Jean. She felt gutted. It was the only evening she'd ever been with him that she feigned tiredness. They left early.

She could still remember the feelings of sheer confusion. Of course she'd never wish for Peter to be in pain, but what about her feelings of despair, annoyance, and frustration?

Her heart suddenly missed a beat. She'd caught sight of a tall, dark-haired figure strolling towards her. For a split second she had been certain it was Peter. Her face turned deathly pale, as though she'd just seen a ghost. It was like being shot through the heart to discover for the umpteenth time that she had mistaken a stranger for Peter.

"Hi! It's a cool morning but at least there's no rain."

The stranger stood next to her and gazed up at the mound.

"Yes," she answered, struggling to regain her composure. "I've been standing here quite a while so the cold is beginning to seep into my bones."

"I'm Sean. Sean Rafter."

"I'm Marion."

The resemblance now that he was up close was not very striking. It had been more of a mirage than a sighting of Peter's double.

"Will you be inside or outside this morning?" He fingered the strap of the black leather bag that hung from his shoulder.

"I'll be inside the cairn, I'm happy to say. And yourself?" She reckoned he must be another journalist. She'd better be careful of what she said.

"Inside. I've got special permission from the powers that be. They've commissioned me to write a guidebook on Newgrange and the satellite monuments. I've always been fascinated by this place. So I'll be scribbling fairly furiously this morning."

He pulled open his bag and took out a large notebook that was filled with all kinds of notes and clippings about Newgrange.

"I've come well prepared as you can see." He fastened his bag again, and searched around in his pocket, finally producing two black pens. "And what about yourself? Are you here for any special reason?"

"If only you knew", she smiled to herself. "I'm awaiting rebirth and transformation at the moment of the solstice!" She quickly searched for a less dramatic explanation.

"I've always been into Irish myths and legends," she said. "And I love the wonderful art work that is dotted all over the cairn. But no, I'm not a writer or anything like that. I'm just here for the experience."

His eyes wondered over the skyline.

"Well, it's still a bit cloudy over the horizon but it's too early to tell yet." Then he yawned, and put a leather-gloved hand over his mouth.

"Sorry. I really feel wrecked. I knew it'd be a mistake to stay out so late. It was my wife's birthday so I had to treat her to a night on the town. When this gig is over I'll be heading back for a few hours kip. Then I'll make a start at typing up today's notes."

He turned his gaze away abruptly. Someone behind must have caught his attention. He waved.

"Oh! It's Nuala. I'd better check in. She's giving me a guided tour of the entire perimeter of the cairn. I'll see you later."

She watched as he entered the enclosure and walked up the path, chatting with Nuala. In the distance he could certainly have passed for Peter. Same height, same build. If only!

It had just gone ten o'clock that night when she'd left him. Since Jim's flat was on her route she called in, on the off chance that he was home. Tonight she really needed a friend. Maybe then the flow of images, words and feelings that kept whizzing around in her brain would somehow be stilled. She was more than relieved to hear the bolt being pulled back and delighted to see Jim's smiling face emerging from behind the sturdy, Georgian door.

"Marion!" he almost roared. "Great to see you. I meant to call you today but this is even better. Come on in! You're just in time for coffee and toast."

It was exactly what she needed: strong coffee, soft music, and a four-seater to lie on. Jim was a great listener. It didn't take him long to suss out the latest scenario.

"You know, I feel he's not right for you, Marion."

She could still hear his words of warning echoing through the early-morning breeze. With Jim there were few frills.

"There may be some chance if he was free and single, but he's been living with that woman for years. So now you tell me he was actually put out of his home for three weeks? And still he tells you they're back in love? Doesn't it all sound just a bit cracked? And I thought my life was mixed up! He's got himself into quite a fix with this Jean. But no matter what, he's still choosing to stick with her. There's nothing wrong with that–commitment, loyalty, and all that, except that you're involved. It seems that you're the fall girl here. I really don't want to see you getting hurt, Marion, but with this guy it seems to be kind of inevitable."

He paused to bite into a slice of hot buttered toast. She nodded. Everything he said made perfect sense.

"He must know you feel a lot for him," he continued. "Why else would you spend so much time with him? You could have anyone you wanted, Marion. I'm not just saying that. It's true. My brother is all the time asking after you. And any of the straight friends I've ever introduced you to always ogle over you. Take the time to look in the mirror someday, okay? You're young, pretty, intelligent and you're choosing to put all your time and energy into Peter. The guy is smart by all accounts. He must know the score."

Jim lay back in his armchair and shook his head slowly. Marion smiled at him weakly. It was good to be reminded that she had something going for her, because up until then she'd felt empty, dried-out, barren.

"I don't doubt that he really likes you," he said. "But, take tonight for instance? He's not the one who's here with you. He's only there when it suits him. That's the way I see it. I'd really love to see you meeting someone special. You deserve the best, Marion. And who knows you better than I do?"

She nodded. Jim was right. But it was all to no avail. Her feelings were too hot and heavy to haul her back from the beckoning chasm.

"There may be no future with Peter, Jim, but there's nothing that compares to being with him. I've never felt this alive before. Deranged, isn't it? My greatest fear is that someday he won't meet me anymore because Jean has got jealous. Even as a friend he means so much to me. If I can only have his friendship then I'll settle for that."

She yawned, then rolled on to her side. She was completely exhausted.

"So it's gone that far." Jim spoke softly. "Would you say you really love him then?"

A deafening silence ensued.

"Yes," she answered. "If there's such a thing as love, then this is it."

He nodded. There was nothing more left to say. He sat watching her as the lamplight lit up her dark, glowing hair.

"You might as well stay where you are. It's too late to stir out. I've loads of duvets. You should be fairly comfortable there."

"Thanks, Jim, for the sofa and for the chat. I really needed to see you tonight."

"Anytime. No problem. Now I'll get you those blankets and let you get to sleep."

She could barely recall a duvet being laid over her, the light being switched off and Jim's voice calling "goodnight!" There was nothing more she knew until morning.

Monday around noon the phone on her desk had blasted her wide-awake. Her stomach did hula-hoops of joy when she heard Peter's voice.

"Well, hello there, Marion. No, I'm not at work because I've picked up a blasted cold. Nothing too serious. I rang in and got the day off. So what about you? Can you meet me for lunch? I'm flexible–anywhere you like. I'm planning to make the most of my sick-day and catch up on some culture. A day in the modern art gallery is just what I need. You're more than welcome if you can get the afternoon off. Just ask. Tell them some sob story about having to bring a relative to the hospital. You're the one who's always on about stained glass and Pre-Raphaelites. Now's your chance to educate Kerrigan. It'll be fantastic. A whole afternoon of refined art, followed by an entire night of crass bars and sordid night-clubs!"

At such short notice it was a miracle she was granted an afternoon's leave. She had been positively purring with sheer unadulterated delight. They had lunched in Cleary's. He was sniffly and a little hoarse, but certainly not a case for the infirmary.

"I needed a day off. I was working on Saturday. It was crazy in there last week. Yesterday Jean went to stay with her sister so I headed home for Ma's Sunday roast. The brother was fooling around with his guitar, trying to put together a new song for his Asylum friends. He had hatched out a fairly good melody but his words were crap. Too bland. Not enough bite. So I gave him a hand. It turned out pretty well, if I may say so myself. It's something that Morrison would have been proud of. Deep, dark and morbid. I've had those words going around in my head for days so they just flowed out, as smooth as a pint of your finest. No, I won't sing it here. Maybe later, if you'll invite me back for a music session!"

"Sure! I can't wait to hear the masterpiece."

She couldn't believe she'd have him all to herself for the whole evening. Hopefully Jean would stay away for a few years!

She had been to the Municipal Art Gallery a few times before. But leave it to Kerrigan to give her a guided tour.

"Here we have a real jewel: Harry Clarke's *The Eve of St. Agnes*. Beautiful isn't it? Look at the detail and the richness of those colours. Pure genius or what? You'll find a lot of his work dotted around the churches all over

Ireland. But needless to say you won't find this kind of sensuality there. Just look at that blonde beauty dressed in her white negligee draped on the edge of the bed! Erotic, isn't it? I'd say you'd look good in something like that yourself! Don't mind me, Marion. It's the art that's gone to my head. In my book, Clarke is our greatest artist."

The reds, blues, yellows and greens streamed like gemstones through the window, falling across his face as he peered into the sparkling glass. Yes, it was magnificent.

"And now for your long awaited Burne-Jones. He was a disciple of the Pre-Raphaelites as far as I remember, but he's close enough. This way, madam!"

He led her to a side chamber. There it was: a full-length canvas of pastel greens and gold. *The Sleeping Princess*, surrounded by her maid servants, each with angelic face and pale, elongated limbs.

"Mm, I'd love to have that in my living room," she laughed.

"Are you inciting me to commit a heinous crime, m'lady?" He poked her teasingly on the arm. "It's good, but I'd rather be sent down for thieving a Rembrandt or a Michelangelo."

He left her pondering the enchanting canvas while he explored the other exhibits.

"Look here!" he pointed to a red board full of steel nails arranged in circles. "I have a thing about so-called modern works of art. That's absolutely pathetic. A kid of three would have more imagination than James Ready, whoever he is. I've seen enough. Are you ready for a drink? I'm parched."

They walked through Parnell Square, down O'Connell Street and into Westmoreland Street. She insisted on stopping off at Bewley's to get a coffee and a sandwich. Then it was down towards Grafton Street in search of a pub. He settled for McDaid's. Not until he was seated and happily sinking into a frothing pint did his tongue become miraculously loosened, especially where the subject of Jean was concerned.

"You're probably sick of me going on about relationship problems but things are still not going great between us."

Marion tried to look sympathetic. It was what she wanted to hear. She felt a mixture of relief and guilt. He continued.

"Most times when we're in the same room it turns into a battlefield. No matter what I do it seems to irritate her. But still, I'm loathed if I'll let go. For most of my adult life I've lived with Jean. I was nineteen when I met her. She was twenty-one. I could never have imagined meeting such a woman—stunning looks, deeply spirited, intelligent, passionate and utterly exhilarating. I wonder what happened to that woman? Come to think of it, I wonder what happened to the man she loved?"

He tried to smile, to hide the pain. Marion felt powerless to help him. It was all too complex, too awful. He sipped his pint and swallowed hard.

"It's all so familiar. Every look of hers conveying a certain mood: the way she fingers her earrings when she's angry, the sound of her laughter, the flash of her eyes, the feel of her skin, the way she used to snuggle up against me when she felt amorous. Hey, I'm getting carried away. Tell me to get lost and sort out my own crap. I deserve it."

"It's okay if you need to talk."

She tried to sound supportive, concerned. Inwardly though she was squirming at the thought of him touching Jean, loving her.

He dragged his fingers carelessly through his hair, then searched for his cigarettes.

"The dream and the reality are epochs apart. I'm not fooling myself."

He lit up a Silk Cut, then automatically reached for

the pint glass resting on the table.

"It's just I feel so stuck, you know what I mean?" He gave her a watery smile. "As long as this situation continues there's no tomorrow. I'm living in this shadowland called yesterday. If it weren't for yourself and the Guinness I'd have sunk without trace months ago. Only for that there would be very little to rouse me from my melancholy. Anyway, you'll get a blast of the old Kerrigan blues later. That song was written straight from the heart, with no holds barred. God knows what Jean will say when she hears it. I'll probably be homeless again!"

She shook her head. She couldn't figure him out. Was there no way of coaxing him away from this mess?

"But why can't you move on if it's causing you so much pain?" She spoke with a mixture of compassion and annoyance.

"No, Marion. From where you're sitting you must think I'm a right glutton for punishment. But you see, in the halcyon days I promised Jean I'd always be there, no matter what happened I'd never leave her. I'm bound to Jean 'till she chooses to sever the umbilical cord. And I really can't expect anyone to understand."

No. He had been right. She hadn't understood then. It sounded so futile, so hopeless. But he was smiling again, at least that was something.

"Anyway, enough of my sordid meanderings. What did you think of Harry Clarke? Impressed? I bet you were..."

It was after eleven when they reached her flat. She made a pot of strong coffee to keep them awake. He turned on the music system. He chose The Beatles.

"I hope you won't mind keeping yourself company while I take a bath." She called to him from the bathroom as she filled the enamel tub with steaming water. "I won't have time in the morning. I know I'll be too exhausted to move."

"Sure, work away. Unless there's an invitation to join you!"

Marion's stomach did somersaults, such was the effect of his words but she recovered in record speed.

"There's more coffee in the pot. Just make yourself at home. I won't be too long."

She always loved her baths: hot, bubbly and aromatic. She added a few drops of lavender and patchouli and then lowered herself into the soft, creamy foam. She closed her eyes and tried to make sense of their connection. Had she been dreaming or had he actually told her in the art gallery that she'd look good in a white negligee? And now he'd just joked about bathing with her. She covered her breasts in soapy suds, and rubbed down her legs with a soft, squishy sponge. Tonight she felt excited, aroused. Just thinking of him sitting there at the other side of the wall, while she lay there naked was deeply erotic, tantalising, thrilling.

She didn't want to keep him waiting too long. She dried herself quickly, then pulled on her purple nightdress, and her black dressing gown. That would have to do. She didn't possess a negligee of any colour. Her hair hung loose and wet around her shoulders. She pushed open the bathroom door. The sound of *Yesterday* and Paul McCartney's soulful voice filled the room. He was lying on the sofa, eyes closed, singing along with his idols.

He half opened his eyes and smiled up at her.

"So how is the bathing beauty?"

"The bath was delicious. Just what I needed."

She sat in an armchair opposite, drying her hair with a towel. It must be the Guinness, she thought, delighted with the complement.

"Turn down the volume, Marion. Before I pass out I'd better sing the famous song I promised. You'll have to imagine the brother's fancy guitar work. Okay? Ready?"

His voice was clear and strong, with no sign of the

afternoon's hoarseness. She listened, entranced. The words were indeed full of despair and darkness. They spoke volumes about his broken world. At some later stage he'd given her a typed copy. She could still recall every verse, every line, every word.

> *Trapped in a cage*
> *At a very young age.*
> *Looking at the night sky*
> *As the lonely years drift slowly by.*
> *He sees no future in the stars*
> *For him there's nothing beyond those prison bars.*

> *Someone help me cries a voice from deep inside his head*
> *Someone end this misery I cannot hide*
> *Someone end this misery inside*
> *Oh Lord! End this misery.*

> *Nothing but an empty shell*
> *Drowning in a wishing well.*
> *Life is a torn out page*
> *Ripped apart in silent rage.*
> *What do you do when sleeps your only friend?*
> *And even then the pain inside it never ends.*

> *Someone help me...*

With eyes closed he sat there, singing his guts out, spilling out the years of pain and shattered dreams.

> *I am innocent!*
> *I am innocent!*
> *But there's nobody listening*
> *The walls have closed their ears*
> *They've heard it all a thousand times before,*
> *They've heard it all a thousand times before.*

He rubbed his eyes and gave her a watery smile. They sat there for what seemed like an eternity in silence, gazing intensely at each other. She spoke at last.

"It's really brilliant, Peter! Well done!"

"Yeah. I believe pain has been the inspiration for all the best songs, the greatest literature, and the most beautiful works of art. They're the most interesting, anyway."

He rubbed his eyes again, yawned, then glanced at his watch.

"You've just had a glimpse of my tattered soul. That's all I can give you tonight, Marion. It's been quite a day and I can barely keep my eyes open. I'm sure you want to hit the hay. And I really need to be up in time for work in the morning. I'll get a taxi at the end of the road. No! I'd better show up tonight or I'll be issued with divorce papers in the morning."

She saw him to the door. The night was clear and the sky was bespeckled with twinkling stars.

"I'll be seeing you!" He waved before turning into the street.

Marion stood in the doorway, following the dark, diminishing figure with her eyes until he was completely lost in blackness.

CHAPTER 9

She glanced towards the mound just in time to spot Nuala and Sean Rafter appearing from behind the quartz facade. Sean was deeply engrossed, furiously scribbling Nuala's anecdotes into his cumbersome notebook. Marion walked alongside the fence, just to stretch her legs. The words and the images inside her head continued to flow, thick and fast...

It was Wednesday around noon when he rang. That phonecall, she'd thought then, was the key to paradise. It was early September. She had kicked her way through leaf-strewn streets of rust, brown and gold. The morning had been mild and sunny. He sounded tired.

"Hi Marion. Life's not been too good. A lot of hassle. All night fights and lack of sleep. Anyway, big changes are finally afoot. I'm starting to look for a new place. I've agreed to be out by the end of the month. The walls have definitely crumbled. At least I'll be free again. It's time I looked at the positive side. I've had enough tears and angry words to last me a lifetime. I'm sick of it."

Her heart missed a beat. Free, at last! Well, it had certainly been on the cards. Her mind was bombarded by a flood of conflicting emotions: sympathy for his understandable pain, delight at the prospect of a future together, excitement tinged with trepidation at the thought of inevitable change.

"I know things have been really difficult for a long time. No one can live with that kind of constant nagging pain. And, as you said, at least you'll be free to make a new life."

She wanted to console him, to soothe his pain, to help him put the past behind him and begin again.

"Yeah, well that's the way I see it now. It's time to recapture some of the old Kerrigan style! Jean will be away next weekend. She's going to stay with her sister in Cork. I'll have the place to myself. I might as well make good use of it. Would you be on for coming over to dinner on Friday evening? Then on Saturday I could show you the local hotspots. There are some fantastic beaches and parks in the area. Maybe we'll have a few music sessions over the weekend. Are you on?"

Suddenly he was all bright and bubbly again. She couldn't believe her ears.

"Sure, Peter. That sounds brilliant. I could meet you after work on Friday." The wedding she'd been invited to on Saturday had suddenly slipped her mind.

"Great! We can meet in Grogan's. Then we can head for Clontarf. We'll celebrate the beginning of a new phase. I'll ring you on Friday so, okay? Talk to you then, Marion."

The thought of being alone with Peter for the weekend both thrilled and scared her. There was no way on earth she'd get sexually involved with him, not until he'd officially finished with Jean. She wasn't even certain if he was physically attracted to her. There was no doubt he liked her. But now that he was free he could have anyone he wanted. Still, there was nothing to be gained in dwelling upon wild speculation. He was finished with Jean and he'd invited her to dinner on Friday evening. Those were the tangible facts.

On Friday at 5.30pm she was sitting in the allotted place, Lucozade in hand, a black, frothing pint on the table in front of her, awaiting his arrival. She wore a pale blue jumper and tight black ski pants. She was beside herself with excitement. She tried to calm herself by focusing on her surroundings. Coloured glass panels added a nice touch to the decor. Paintings lined the walls, many of them for sale. Grogan's was noted for its bohemian and artistic clientele.

"I love this place," he'd said, the first night he'd brought her there. "The people who drink here aren't pretentious. They like drawing and painting. It's that simple. They don't need to make a song and dance about it."

The pub was filling up with various workers arriving for their Friday evening drinks. Her face broke into a wide grin when she spotted him.

"Hello there. It's warm isn't it? Ah! The lady has even bought me a pint? Things are looking up." There was no place in the world she'd rather be at this precise moment than sitting here with Peter Kerrigan.

"I'm out to paint the town red tonight. Are you on?"

He barely mentioned the pending split. She figured he was trying hard to erase it from his mind. He'd gone through enough reminiscing in the last few weeks, he said, to last a lifetime. She was delighted to see him in good spirits again. He was mellow, laid back, all smiles. She soon lost count of the number of times he'd gone to the bar, but he must have knocked back at least six pints in rapid succession. His packet of Silk Cut was also rapidly diminishing. It was no wonder he laughed at life, the universe and everything.

"Take it all in your stride, Marion. Be happy. Don't worry!"

It was after ten when they left the pub.

"What about some food, then music? We're free agents, Marion. It's a long time since I've felt like this. I don't really give a damn what anyone thinks." He staggered down the road, waving his arms in the air, singing with gusto.

It's years since I've seen the night sky
And its myriad of stars

Without being walled-in
Behind those iron bars.

"Forget Morrison", he shouted. "Kerrigan is the new blues king!"

He led her to a Greek restaurant in Wicklow Street. He ordered a bottle of wine. They ate hummus, a delicious salad and a selection of other weird and wonderful fare.

"I have a real love of Greece." He breathed in the aroma of the wine then took a long slow sip. "The people, the sun, the beaches, the culture, the booze and the food. Who could ask for more? I'm planning on taking a trip there later in the year. I might go alone. Or maybe you'd like to come along with me?"

Her face flushed with delight. "I'd love to!" She couldn't believe how quickly it was all happening.

"Right!" he winked over at her. "Now let me pay the bill. Then to J.J. Smyth's for some real blues."

It was a brilliant night. The sound of the sax and the screaming guitars made her dizzy. She met a few college friends. He met Michelle, an old flame. Later he told her she had a special place in his past. She was the first girl he'd ever slept with. Marion sat watching as the tall, redhead tried to rekindle the spark. She was all over him, with one hand rubbing his knee and the other feeling his thigh. Michelle certainly looked overwhelming, with her enormous shoulder-padded jacket, her huge dangling earrings, her lace, fingerless gloves and her tight leather skirt.

"Time to go, Marion." He shouted across the table, as he tried to prise Octopus Michelle away from him. "It's the same old story. These women can never keep their hands off me! It must be the Kerrigan charm. I'm dead beat anyway. Yeah, nice seeing you again, Michelle." He dodged her pursed lips and made a run for the door. "Marion, are you coming to Clontarf?"

Michelle let out a stream of obscenities as Marion fled the scene. She was more than relieved to feel the cool night air on her face. He was full of apologies.

"Sorry about that. She's not a bad kid really. The drink has probably gone to her head. Taxi!"

She loved night-time Dublin. It always made her feel so alive. She stared out of the side window. The reflection of the coloured lights on the Liffey and all along the seafront looked wonderful, romantic.

"Next turn left. Then it's home, or it used to be home, I should say."

It was a large, semi-detached, two-storey house with a small garden in front. He opened the door and led her inside. It was simply decorated. Pale colours on the walls: cream, beige, peach, and blue. Quite sparse. No clutter. Jean had very different taste from her own. There was a tall cheese plant in the hall. The main features in the sitting room were a big soft chair and a three-seater sofa. A built-in unit contained their state-of-the-art music system. She had never seen such a huge collection of records, tapes and CDs. There was also a large bookcase, full to the brim. The carpet was a mixture of grey, blue and white. The only picture on the wall was yet another photograph of Jean, walking along the seashore, her golden hair sailing in the wind.

"And now for some music! Make yourself at home. Coffee?" He was the perfect host.

She sat on the sofa. It was 1am. She felt really tired. She took off her shoes and curled up in the soft folds. The sound of Jethro Tull flowed over her. She closed her eyes. She heard him rattling cups and pouring coffee.

"Not falling asleep on me, I hope. It could be a long night yet."

He handed her a steaming mug.

"I feel so tired," she yawned.

"Well, there's no shortage of beds here." He paused and sipped his coffee. He was looking at her intensely.

"Do you want your own bed, or do you want to share a bed?"

Her stomach tightened. She was speechless.

"I think I'll stay here." She answered shyly.

"Cop out!" he smiled. "I've spent many a night on that sofa myself over the last few months. I haven't bothered to sleep upstairs in quite a while."

So he hadn't been sleeping with Jean. The fact remained that he still lived with her. She drank the strong coffee and then closed her eyes again. He stretched out his hand and pulled her up from the sofa.

"There's a spare bed upstairs. You might as well be comfortable."

Maybe he had only been joking. She was too tired to figure it out. Within seconds of touching the pillow she was asleep.

She awoke to the streaming sunlight. Where was she? Oh yes, in Kerrigan's lair! The room was quite small. The walls were pale blue. The bed was covered with a lemon quilt and there was a cream built-in wardrobe in the far corner. He was knocking on the door.

"Marion. It's nearly twelve. Come down for breakfast."

"Okay! I'm on my way."

She really felt like lounging in a hot, soapy bath. She opened the door to her left. A king-sized brass bed took up most of the space. The cover was all crumpled. It must have been their bedroom. She closed the door quietly. When she found the bathroom she wrapped herself in a huge towel and walked downstairs.

"Good morning! Yes I slept fine. Is it all right if I have a bath?"

She noticed him glancing at her legs. She felt all quivery inside.

"Of course. The water should be hot."

She felt his eyes all over her as she climbed the stairs.

He was still standing there, gazing after her when she closed the bathroom door. She began running the water. She examined the bottles and containers on the wooden shelf. This was Jean's vanilla shampoo and Jean's apple soap. Well, she needed to use them this morning so there was no point in being coy.

He was sitting in the garden when she came down. He wore a check shirt, open at the neck, and a pair of black denims.

"There's a pot of coffee and some home-made bread on the table. Bring it out here if you like. It's beautiful. I admit I'm a sun worshipper. By the way, I made the bread."

"Imagine if every morning could be like this", she thought. "Imagine if this was their home. Imagine if he loved her."

Her hair had grown long and wavy in the last few months. She sat on the rug he'd laid out for her, teasing out the wet strands with her fingers, relishing the warmth of the sun. She balanced a plate of bread on her knee and held a mug of creamy coffee in her hand. She was aware of him watching her. She knew he liked her without make-up. He'd told her she looked young and fresh, uncomplicated and free. She smiled over at him. He looked tired and drawn. Maybe he had a sore head from all the drink the night before.

"Those purple flowers are beautiful," she gestured towards a flower basket. "I love this time of year."

He nodded. She wondered what he was thinking. Maybe she could help him end the pain.

They spent the entire day walking for miles along golden beaches. This was her favourite place. The sea was vast, never-ending. She stopped to throw stones, to watch the ripples spiral to infinity. The ebb and the flow stilled her mind.

"It's a spiritual experience," she laughed.

She met his gaze. He smiled.

"It's a good place to ponder your life, if that's what you mean."

He bent down to pick up a stick and then threw it far out to sea.

"To get some kind of clarity on your mistakes, to laugh at life's absurdity. We're dots, Marion. A dot on a rock, on a coast, on a planet, on a solar system. For dots we have fairly high opinions of ourselves."

They climbed over ditches. They walked along paths and then they came to a green oasis. She had no idea where they were. This was unknown territory. But Peter knew every inch of the place.

"St. Ann's Park, Raheny. The rose gardens here are world famous. In autumn they should be in full bloom. I suppose they're special but I prefer the wide-open fields myself. This way."

An overhead trellis, entwined with roses, announced the entrance to the gardens. The scent was delicate, sweet, and unmistakably rose. This was her favourite flower. It had everything to excite the senses: an intoxicating aroma, a soft velvety touch and colours to set the world spinning: blood red, pale pink, ivory and sun-kissed yellow.

Within seconds of their arrival the sky burst open and rain poured down in buckets. They ran to seek shelter under the trellis.

"Autumn showers. It shouldn't last long." Peter buttoned his coat and pulled up his collar. "I remember being stuck on a mountain in Scotland once and it absolutely rained in torrents. There wasn't a stick of shelter. I was with the sister at the time. We were completely drowned."

Raindrops flowed through the holes in the trellis. They were both soaking.

"When you desire a day in the depths of nature you must be prepared for the whimsical moods of the elements." He shook the heavy drops from his hair.

They were standing side by side. She was aware of their arms touching. If only he would hold her. But he made no move to touch her.

In minutes the sun broke through the clouds and they ran from their hiding place. The drops of water sitting on the petals sparkled like jewels.

"I wish I had my camera," she sighed.

That was one thing she always regretted. There was no photo of them together in existence. It probably summed up the strangeness of their connection.

They stopped off at a pub for a drink. She was starving but he wouldn't let her eat anything.

"I'm making dinner, remember? Okay so I never got around to it last night, but we'll make up for it tonight. It's better when your hunger has an edge to it."

That didn't stop him from drinking his Guinness. He sat watching her, all smiles. Her hair and face were streaked with blue, green, yellow and red, where the sunlight burst through the stained glass windows above.

"She comes in colours," he sang. He couldn't stop smiling. "You know what, Marion?" He placed his hand lightly on her arm. "Things are really looking up!"

It was after eight when they returned to Clontarf.

"I'll get chopping. Curry and rice, is that okay?"

He turned on the tape deck. At the touch of a button the sound of seagulls soared through the room: *The lonesome boatman.* He went to his bookcase.

"You can amuse yourself with this. It's quite informative."

He handed her a large, hard-backed volume, *An Interpretation of the Artwork of Newgrange.* She flicked through the pages. There were the spirals and lozenge shapes decorating the entrance stone, the passageway and the kerb. She could still remember the main gist of the text it had fascinated her so much:

...The spiral symbolises the natural form of growth.

In all cultures it is the symbol of eternal life. The great flowing whorls represent the continuous creation and dissolution of the world, the constant movement between life, death and rebirth. The entrance stone at Newgrange is covered with spirals. It restricts access to the megalithic tomb, to the other world. This was a necessary passport in the sacred dance, through the labyrinth, to the hidden realms within. Only the initiated, those specially chosen for their spiritual wisdom, were allowed entry…

"I'm leaving it to simmer. It shouldn't take too long. Here's some salad as a starter."

She put down the book and helped him to lay the table. It was all so intimate. He filled his own glass with wine. She poured chilled water into hers.

"Slainte!"

"Cheers, Peter!"

It was a really good meal. After all that fresh air she had been ravenous. The curry was hot and spicy, the way she liked it. His talents seemed to know no bounds.

"I certainly won't starve when I'm living alone," he joked.

She wondered what he was feeling. She couldn't even imagine how bad it would feel to lose a home. Was he really broken-hearted underneath it all? She remembered when she'd split with John. There had been a lot of pain and rejection. And she hadn't even slept with him, let alone shared her life with him.

Later that evening when they were sitting in the living room listening to The Moody Blues, she saw him wipe a tear from his eye.

"Sorry. *Nights in White Satin* always reminds me of Jean. It brings me back to the early days: living in a tiny bed-sit, sitting up half the night smoking dope, playing all those psychedelic songs, making love for hours on end. All that love. And in the end it meant nothing."

Marion didn't want to see his pain. If he could only put it behind him then maybe there could be a chance of happiness. She was sitting at his feet, gazing up into his eyes.

"I'm not the messiah, Marion. I don't have all the answers. Be the centre of your own universe, not someone else's satellite." He looked at her with tired eyes. "It's probably the drink that's brought on the sentiment. But I'm not even drunk yet. You wouldn't know anything about it but when you drink to a certain point it deadens the pain."

He sat for a long time, eyes closed, stretched out on the floor. The music played on. She curled herself up on the sofa again. It had been a long, strange day. She felt worn out.

"Marion, don't fall asleep. We could make love if you like."

She wasn't sure she'd heard him correctly. Her face had either turned white or red, she didn't know which. She felt confused. She didn't answer. He shrugged his shoulders.

"It's early yet," he yawned.

He closed his eyes again. A few minutes later he was breathing deeply. She tiptoed upstairs, got into bed and fell fast asleep.

She yawned and stretched her arms upwards. She was getting a little impatient now. She'd love to gain admission to the site, to walk around the cairn, to trace the smooth flowing spirals with her fingers. That would be a good way to prepare for the dawning of a new day, a new year, a new life. She glanced at the people behind her. There must be sixty or seventy now. No sign of Red Nuala unlocking the gate yet. She could unravel another coil, trace another spiral in the recesses of her mind...

"I've spent the entire week combing the 'Flats for let' section of every newspaper. Some of the places I've seen leave a lot to be desired and the prices are astronomical.

But I've managed to get a place that's fairly decent. It's in Terenure. The next turn left after the church. It's a separate living room, kitchen, bedroom and bathroom. The main perk is that it has an open fire. I'm moving in at the weekend. Jean is helping me move most of my stuff. It's quite amicable between us now. We've decided to remain friends. She's giving me a lot of stuff to kit out the place: pots, pans, cutlery, that kind of thing. The stereo and the TV are mine. She's keeping the house. Well, we've both paid the mortgage but her folks gave her the deposit so...but anyway I wouldn't like to take it from her. I'll get something out of it. Besides that, it's a new start."

He sounded bright and positive. It was great he was taking it this way.

"So I'll have a flat warming on Wednesday evening. You'd better be there. If you've a friend coming to stay that's no problem. Bring her along too. We won't exclude her because she's an accountant. We can deal with that. I'm just asking a few friends over on different evenings. It's better that way than trying to unite the many diverse aspects of my crazy life. And I'll be doing the rounds of the markets too, if you'd like to come along. I'm looking for a big rug and a few wall hangings. You'd probably have a good eye for that kind of thing."

Marion was beaming. All of a sudden the whole world opened up in vivid technicolour. A giant kaleidoscopic rainbow lit the sky. The path was clear. She was now at the centre of his life.

"Orla is due to arrive at 6.30 on Wednesday", she explained. "We'll need to get something to eat. I was thinking of Pizzaland. Sure, Peter. That sounds fine. We'll meet you there. I'll be going home this weekend but next week if you need a hand with anything just ask. I'm certainly available for any market expeditions. I love browsing around Mother Redcaps. I have a good eye for a bargain too!"

He was already inspecting the menu when they arrived. Orla had been her flat mate for a year in college. She was now living in Galway with her husband, Paul. She was staying in Dublin with Marion while she did a two-day tax refresher course.

"Hello Peter." Orla shook his outstretched hand. "Marion has told me all about you. A '60s man! When we were staying together in Stillorgan we were famous for our 'hippie' music belting out all over the estate. We had some great times then. So you work with computers?"

He was in top form that evening.

"Well, don't hold that against me, Orla! A man has to earn a buck. At least computers are logical. If there's a problem there's always a definite solution. Now, people! That's another story." He turned to Marion. "I don't think I'd like the job of helping people solve their problems. Sometimes there mightn't be a solution. The person just might have to go through that particular experience no matter how potentially destructive, to get to a new level of awareness, perhaps years later. I don't envy the psychologist's job for a second."

Marion found it difficult to answer this one. She saw the psychologist's role as supporting, encouraging, gently challenging. Unless you were invited to enter another person's world you had no right to be there. And it was true: sometimes people refused any kind of support.

"Everyone needs help at some time in their lives." Marion looked directly at Peter. "Some people are lucky enough to have supportive partners, family or friends. But there are times when things go badly wrong and then it's time to call in a trained professional. That's the way I see it anyway. And there are always those who refuse all help and go it alone. That's a valid choice too."

"Yeah, sure. As I read somewhere once: 'Life's a bitch and then you die!' Not too promising for humanity, is it?" He turned to Orla again. "Marion tells me you're married. But you look so young! Twenty-five maybe? It always intrigues me how people can have so much faith in another human being to actually commit themselves for life."

He had set the cat among the pigeons. The waitress came over to the table and they ordered.

"I met my husband in college. Marion was with me, at Cleo's party. We just kind of clicked. We liked the same music. We both loved to travel. We felt this huge attraction towards each other. He's a great guy. After college we both looked for work in Galway. It was his home and I loved the place. We lived together for a year and then decided–this is it! We're both very happy." Orla fingered the gleaming diamond on her left hand.

"Well isn't that lovely!" Peter put on a real sickly-sweet voice. "If life could only be that simple for all of us. When things are going great it's all rosy in the garden. The problem is we really believe we know the other person inside out. Most people foolishly think they have a claim on their partner's life. We haven't moved very far from the days of chattels and possessions. A woman is *given away* by her father to her husband. She then wears a ring, a symbol that she is bound to love, honour and *obey* her husband. Aren't they the sacred vows? It's more than likely she'll go the full hog and abandon her former identity by accepting her husband's name. And they believe they are one, in body and soul! That's a complete fallacy. The reality is we never know anyone. That's the golden rule. People change. It's usually subtle but then again it can happen overnight. We talk of love, when we really mean need. We want someone to make us happy, to give us sex when we're horny, to cuddle us when we're lonely and to reassure us when we're despondent. We want to be special, to be number one in at least one person's eyes. So much of so-called love is me, me, me!"

He paused for a sip of wine. Orla stared at him with her mouth agape. Peter was certainly wound up and he hadn't finished yet.

"Not to be totally cynical, there are times when we would die for the other person, we feel so much love. But that's because the thought of living without the beloved is so desperate. Living without that feeling of being loved, of being capable of giving pleasure, of being part of something bigger than yourself can be unbearable. But it's the truth. We are all alone."

Orla was too taken aback to speak. Another Kerrigan listener to be struck down with a pounding headache. At best, Orla looked shocked, a little embarrassed or maybe angry. Marion had heard much of this before. She didn't like it when he spoke about love as a need. It wasn't exactly romantic. The more she thought about it though the more she saw his point. And allowances had to be made for him. He had just split up with Jean after eight years. He was disillusioned and in considerable pain. That was understandable.

At that precise moment Niamh arrived. Orla sat facing her, chatting. Peter was opposite Marion.

"Okay, enough about love, sex and heartache. After we finish here we can go for a quick drink. Maybe we'll hit The Palace Bar. I met Jean there on Sunday night. Ah, it went okay. Then later she came over to inspect the flat. We ordered pizza, watched a video. It was weird really, to be entertaining Jean like some acquaintance. But we've got to move on. We have to pull ourselves out of the mire. At least we're still friends. Anyway, tonight I'm a free man. In many ways that feels really good. You've no idea what it's like to constantly have to anticipate someone else's reaction, if you do this or that. It's like walking barefoot over red-hot coals. There's no way you can escape being burned."

One drink in The Palace Bar soon turned into six. It was nearly twelve before they got to Terenure. It was a basement flat, with its own entrance. In the main room there was an open fire, a sofa that could double up as a bed, and two armchairs. His music system and bookcase occupied centre stage. There was also a small kitchen and a bathroom. He pointed to another door.

"That's the bedroom," he said, looking at Marion.

They sat up half the night, switching the tape deck from Bowie to Lynott, and from Dillon to Marley. Peter produced a bottle of whiskey. His friends, Joc and Marie, had called over the evening before and had presented him with this treasured gift. Niamh and Orla tried a glass. Marion stuck to mineral water. At four in the morning communal sleep descended. Peter fought hard to rouse himself to call a taxi.

"You could stay, if you wanted to." He glanced at Marion, through blood-shot, weary eyes. "This girl could have me if she liked," he announced to the general gathering, and then winked at Marion. She was speechless. "Yes, you're right. Wait 'till I'm sober."

She felt a wave of annoyance rush over her. "Well, top marks for subtlety, Peter!" Maybe he was joking, teasing her, while all along he didn't mean a word of it? With that thought the doorbell rang and they fell out into the cold night air.

He called over early on Sunday. It was a mild October day. They strolled along Clanbrassil Street, stopping off to admire the architectural splendour of St. Patrick's Cathedral, then left into Meath Street. The markets were in full swing. Stalls were crammed with food, clothes and bric-a-brac.

"Nothing much here, Marion. It's only a load of junk. Let's try Mother Redcaps."

This was much more up-market: antiques, African soapstone sculptures, Mexican silver, Moroccan pottery, Indian silks, and a large selection of Turkish rugs. Peter chose two Egyptian papyrus paintings and a large soft, black rug.

"Let's go for a coffee. Then I'll really have to get these things back to the flat. I don't fancy lugging them around all day. I'd hoped we'd have time to fit in *the real* art gallery, not the modern one. It's ages since I've visited the Dutch masters. Plan B would involve a walk in Bushy Park. Have you been there yet? No? It's really something else. We'll have to hurry so, before it gets dark. Forget the coffee. Taxi!"

It was indeed a wonderful place, a mini forest, complete with stream and old stone bridge. There was even a football field, a playing area for kids, a bandstand and tennis courts. Marion loved playing tennis. Now she knew where to bring her cousin, Mike, the next time he came to stay. The trees were almost bare. The light was fading to silvery-grey. The pond was full of ducks and sweeping seagulls. Four beautiful white swans glided over to where they were standing.

"Hey, look at the children of Lir!" Peter pointed. "You'd never know who'd turn up in this enchanted place. It's a pity we didn't bring some bread. Not a bad replacement for my back garden, is it?"

They walked among the trees until dusk. He told her of the bands he'd love to bring her to, the day trip they could take to Newgrange and the weekend they could spend touring Donegal. This was the county he'd spent two summers in as a child. An eccentric aunt had rented a cottage there to do some writing and had allowed her niece and nephews to visit for a few weeks. The weeks had turned into months. That was the best time of his life, he said, so far.

They stepped along a line of flat boulders that crossed the Dodder. Peter was weighted down by shopping bags after the market expedition but he didn't seem to care.

"I'll make us dinner. I'm starving. Anything in particular you fancy, Marion?" He couldn't have been more obliging. "And we can get a video. Is there anything special you'd like to see?"

See chose *Lady Hawk*. Jim had recommended it. It

was set in medieval times, full of magic, sword fights, chivalrous heroes and virtuous maidens. She hadn't realised the leading lady was Michelle Pfeiffer. She hoped Peter wouldn't notice the resemblance, between Michelle and Jean.

When they arrived at his place he made coffee and switched on the music system. *Brothers in Arms* played softly in the background. He began to cook pasta. He served it with crispy rolls and a beautiful cheese sauce. Her contribution was to set the table and wash the dishes. Afterwards she lay on the sofa. He put some coal on the fire. Then he sat on the floor, philosophising and changing tapes. There was a cosy intimacy between them.

"Are you tired?" he asked. "We can watch that movie another night."

She half-opened her eyes. He'd lit the small lamp. The fire crackled in the heart. Everything was perfect.

"Yes. I think I'm falling asleep," she answered lazily.

"You can sleep here if you like. Or there's a bed inside."

He spoke softly, staring over as she lay there.

"This will do fine. If you have a few blankets, I'll just throw them over me." She sat there gazing at him in the half-light.

He shrugged his shoulders. "It's your choice, Marion."

He disappeared and came back a few minutes later carrying a duvet, blankets and pillows. He placed the pillows under her head and covered her up with the blankets.

"See you in the morning," he said. "I'll leave some music playing to put you to sleep. Pleasant dreams."

She lost consciousness somewhere in the middle of, *He ain't heavy.*

That time was all a whirl. About three months it

lasted. They went to The Screen and The Lighthouse. He liked foreign films. She remembered one of the tragic love stories, set in South America: two star-crossed lovers caught up in the throes of political and social turmoil. They went to The Abbey and The Gate. *The Crucible*, the story of the Salem witch trials was powerful stuff. They went drinking in the Old Dubliner, The Fogey Dew, The International Bar, and The Norseman. They were at all the main gigs. The highlight was when he bought her a ticket for Mark Knopfler. It was a fantastic experience. They danced side by side to *Sultans of swing* and *Romeo and Juliet*. It was her turn to wipe away the tears.

For Romeo and Juliet, there was no doubt that the timing had been all wrong. Marion dearly hoped that her stars and those of Peter's were perfectly aligned, blessed by the heavens, truly in the ascendant.

CHAPTER 10

The chill was beginning to seep into her bones. She rubbed her hands together. There was still no movement at the gate. She returned to her reverie, allowing the drama to unfold...

All that was two years ago; just before she had accompanied Jim and the gang to Newgrange, when there'd all been turned away. She'd spent that Christmas with her family. There was plenty of time to dwell on Peter. Being away from him for over a week brought her to boiling point. She was starved, ravenous. She found herself waking in the middle of the night, wet and feverish. Dreams of gentle kisses all over her skin, and long sliding fingers undressing her, filled her fretful sleep. His face was permanently etched on her mind.

He'd called the first day she was back at work. He sounded eager to meet that evening. The plan was to call into O'Donoghue's, then to have dinner back at his place.

He was sitting at the bar, sipping a beer when she arrived. He was all smiles, simply radiating warmth. She asked how the holidays went.

"Okay. Nothing spectacular. I spent a few days with the folks at home. Then I went to Clare for New Year's. Joe and Marie have a holiday home there. It was good fun. Anything wild yourself?"

She told him that Christmas had been very quiet. "I

missed our chats", she said, feeling shy and awkward.

"You missed the old Kerrigan charm then?" He gave her an intense look. "It's over two years now since we've known each other. We've been through all kinds of stuff together. Which of us do you think knows the other best?"

She felt she knew everything there was to know about him, though she wondered how well he really knew her. He was the talker, often wearing his heart on his sleeve. She was the listener, the observer. When he'd had a few drinks he certainly had little problem letting his emotions flow.

"I'd say I know you very well," she replied.

"Maybe you can see into my deepest soul, Marion! But the main thing is that we really like each other." He looked directly into her eyes. "And for me, when you really like someone, as well as fancying her, then the sexual thing usually raises its head. If you'll pardon the pun!"

He scrutinised her face, searching for an answer.

"You can stay with me tonight, if you like", he said, his dark eyes boring into her. "You can leave a spare toothbrush over in my place in future. You needn't bother with a nightdress. You won't be cold. I'll keep you warm, Marion. I'm not even asking you to have sex. Though if you want to, I've no objection! Hugs and kisses will be a good start. I'm good in that department too."

At long last he'd said it. She felt a quivering sensation all along her stomach, her thighs and somewhere deep inside her. She was speechless. He shrugged his shoulders and smiled weakly, wondering what she was thinking.

"Okay, Peter!" she answered at last.

He pushed his half-filled pint aside, grabbed his jacket from the back of the chair and asked her if she was ready.

"We won't bother with the lights. I'll make up a big fire. I've got some candles I've been meaning to light. Will you do the honours?"

She lit the four candles with shaking hands. This was all so strange. She felt as though she was sleepwalking, moving in a kind of daze. There was some unknown part of her emerging, naturally surfacing. The time had come. Thinking back to that night, for a man who wasn't a believer in God, religion or spirituality, he certainly had a sixth sense for creating the perfect scene for the enactment of an ancient ritual. Of course there had to be music: slow, rhythmic, deep and swirling.

"Are we bedding it?" he almost whispered.

She followed him into the bedroom. She scrambled onto the bed. She pulled off her cardigan, her dress and tights. She placed them on a chair and snuggled down under the covers. A small lamp was lighting. He'd left the music on in the living room. He got undressed. He was naked. She tried not to stare but he was beautiful.

"This is exciting," he smiled, trying to make her feel at ease.

He turned off the light. In the darkness she felt him edging closer. She felt his mouth on hers and they kissed, long and passionate. He wrapped his arms around her and hugged her tightly. She felt herself slipping, falling into a deep, dark ocean, scared, yet wildly exhilarated. He slid his hands slowly down her body, freeing her from the last vestments of clothing. He gently rubbed her breasts, stroked her stomach and thighs.

It wasn't 'till he told her he wanted to make love that she whispered it was her first time.

"Don't be scared," he said. "Trust me. I'll make sure you're safe."

He licked and kissed every inch of her body. There were sounds that she'd never imagined coming from deep inside her, strange, earthy sounds. Hot shuddering tremors flowed in waves along her spine. She didn't recognise herself, let alone the man who pulled her tightly to him, an urgency to open her body, to connect, not through words, but in some ancient, primal way.

After that night she would never be the same again. A missing link had been fitted into place. There was a new understanding of life, of people, of herself.

"You did it!"

He kissed her on the lips. He wrapped his legs around hers. He pulled her head onto his chest. He held his arms locked around her neck. He stroked her hair. She heard his heart racing. In moments he was asleep.

It took her hours to doze. She still couldn't believe it was true. She felt his body against hers. All her life there had been such loneliness. There were family and friends who she dearly loved, but this was different. Touch was the difference. She had been starved of touch. He often said this to her. He could feel it in her kisses and in her fingers. She was like a child, searching, curious, a foreigner in her own land.

Every time she was with him she could feel her barriers disintegrating. Like a glass being smashed, splintering into trillions of pieces, scattering at random to the four corners of the earth. It was total demolition of self, melting into a unity of flesh, bone, skin, and spirit, all in slow motion. Invariably the reel of film would rewind, all the amputated pieces flowed back together, raised up from the floor, magnetically drawn to reform the whole. Her glass walls closed in again. She was alone.

Next morning he made breakfast. They were separate again. He didn't touch her. In between sips of coffee he kept looking at her. She tried to talk about everyday things. It hadn't dawned on her yet that their friendship had ended. The earthquake of the previous night had changed all that.

They were both late for work. She didn't want to

leave him. The only good thing about it was that she could ring her friends and tell them the news. For the first time in her life she felt wanted, beautiful. At long last she had found someone who loved her...

"Hello there, Miss. Sorry for disturbing you. Beautiful, isn't it?"

Talk about bad timing! Here she was, revelling in the most passionate night of her life and this guy comes sticking his nose in!

"What is it you want?" she sounded annoyed. Her face was quite flushed. He was like someone from another planet, as far as she was concerned: thin grey hair, slightly balding, large stomach protruding over his trousers, large black sack on his back, tripod in hand.

"I'm with the press. Alan Crowley at your service. I'll be in the chamber at dawn to hopefully capture the sun's entrance. Nuala was telling me you'll be there too. I just wanted to ask your permission, if the light is at the right angle and you're in the right position, can I snap your picture? Then if it's what we're looking for we'll publish it in tomorrow's edition."

Marion stood staring at him.

"My picture? Why do you want to take my picture?" she asked in amazement.

He pulled the sack higher on his shoulder. "Well, Miss, you're exactly what I'm looking for. I just spotted you standing there, gazing at the mound. Nuala says you can move up front, just to make sure you're in the firing line, so to speak."

She had to smile at his audacity. She really didn't care much at that particular moment who took her picture.

"If you feel that inspired then go ahead." She gave him a faint smile.

He cackled, delighted with himself, thanked her and then left her alone.

A thought crashed into her mind. "If her photo appeared in tomorrow's paper, would he see it?" The day she could experience anything and feel completely indifferent as to whether or not he ever got to hear about it would be a giant leap forward. But she obviously hadn't reached that point yet. She began to pace again along the fence. Her mind flashed to the next scene...

It was two days later when she'd rang him. She had been gliding on air. Dreaming of nights of bliss in bed with her dark-haired lover and days spent rambling through ancient ruins, theorising and laughing, all to the sound of the '60s beat. She'd received no roses. No lover's note.

"Hello Peter." She tried to sound calm, normal.

"Hi!" He sounded low. She felt a ball of tension form in the pit of her stomach. "It's really busy here today", he said. "How are things with you?"

"Okay, busy too." She tried to hide the feeling of anxiety that was running rampant all over her body. "I was just wondering if you'd like to meet up after work." She held her breath.

"No. Not tonight, Marion. I just need to have a bit of space. I need to sort some things out in my head."

She couldn't believe what she was hearing. "I'd really like to see you," she said, trying to hide her desperation, a horrible feeling of panic flooding her mind.

"I just need to spend some time alone, Marion. I haven't done that in a very long time. We can meet up if you like at the weekend."

She tried to be reasonable. He had a right to be by himself sometimes. He had refused to meet her before but then it was different. Now she felt this overwhelming need: to be with him was everything.

"Well, if you don't want to meet me there's nothing I can do." She was trying not to cry. The disappointment was crushing her.

"I'll ring you on Friday. I'll probably feel much better then. It's just that so much is happening so quickly. Okay?" She knew he was trying to placate her. She had little choice but to go along with it.

"Okay. We can meet on Saturday then?" She clung to any straw she could find.

"Yeah, we'll meet on Saturday. I'd better go here. Take care. Bye."

The pain was crippling. It was impossible to function, to eat or to sleep, to work or to live when she wasn't sure whether or not she'd see him. Almost the whole of last year had been like that, filled with uncertainty. There had been so many extremes of emotion. The pure rapture of being with him; then she'd forget the pain and the fear that she was losing herself. She would deny all those feelings to have a chance of meeting him. Love and desire pushed her onwards towards destruction and inevitable doom. The free, unfettered, balanced, in-control woman had vanished. A stranger, unknown even to herself, lay slumped in her place.

She called to his flat that Saturday. They had arrange to meet at 2pm. She hadn't slept a wink. The thought of being with him was all consuming. She wanted to run, to wrap herself around him and kiss him passionately. He opened the door and she walked inside. He was watching a tennis match. It took hours for them to speak their truths. The weather, the soccer scores, nothing but small talk. He asked if she'd like to go for a walk. It was rush hour. Everyone was scurrying home with bulging bags and screaming kids. They stopped for a drink in Cassidy's.

"White lemonade, is that okay?"

"Fine!"

She sat at a table at the back of the pub. She was

shaking. He returned with the drinks. He took a few sips before he spoke.

"I'm sorry, Marion, if you've felt I've been messing you around. I never meant for that to happen. You're the only real friend I've got."

He took a long drink then brushed his hand across his mouth. She watched his every move. Those were the same hands that had stroked and caressed her only nights before. How could all that have changed so suddenly?

"I really like you. I enjoy your company. I'm attracted to you, not just physically but as a whole person". He lit up a Silk Cut and inhaled, then exhaled a billow of smoke. "While I was with Jean I didn't want anything like this to happen. Maybe it was a bit premature the other night, but when two people are hot for each other, then bang!"

He smiled for the first time that day. "I'm being completely honest with you, Marion. I've reached a watershed in my life, a crossroads. I've no idea where I'm going or what direction my life will take. Sometimes there's a blackness, that's all I can see, blackness, and other times its okay."

He took another mouthful of beer. "I know it was a major thing for you…what we did the other night. Any guy would have jumped at the chance to be with you. It's just I can't be sure about anything anymore. Once I thought I had my whole life moving on an even keel. I was wrong. Now I'm left with sheaths of disillusionment, layers of pain and broken dreams, all seeping down through the cracks of my mind. I feel old, Marion. Old and tired."

He paused for more liquor.

"Is it Jean?" She needed to know if he still held out any chance of being with her.

"Not now!" He shook his head. "There was a time when everything I did concerned Jean, but that's over. You're an important part of my life, Marion. But I've been through all kinds of stuff in the last few years. I'm not the man I was. I've lost so much. Not just Jean, but dreams, ideals, values. I need to recharge myself. I just can't be there for someone all the time. I'm going to need space to get my life back on track. It'll take all the energy I have simply to exist."

She was glued to his every word. She didn't dare take her eyes off him in case he might vanish into thin air.

"I love you," she said. That was her simple truth.

"I don't know what love is anymore." He'd said it. It stung her. "I like you a lot. That's the most I can feel for anyone at the moment. I'm being honest, Marion. I've no time for dishonesty."

Silence fell over their table. Voices laughed and chatted all around them. They each sipped their drinks. He stumped out one cigarette, then immediately lit up another.

"I don't know if I'll ever live with anyone again," he continued. "I've just split up from one relationship. I lost my home. I lost practically everything. I don't know if I'll ever risk that again. Hanging your life on someone else's feelings isn't an intelligent way to live, or so I've discovered, the hard way."

She didn't understand him. She only knew how she felt and what she wanted. If it wasn't love he felt for her, then what was it?

"What I'm saying is, I can't promise you anything, Marion. I could make up all kinds of things, but I wouldn't do that to you." His eyes were boring into hers. He looked sad and tired.

They walked back to his flat. He kept watching her. She was hunched up like a woman condemned. He prepared dinner, something quick and tasty. He turned on the music system. Dylan's *Just like a woman* filled the room. He placed several logs on the fire. Within seconds the flames danced and crackled in the grate. She lay on the sofa. She was exhausted. He turned off the lights and sat on the floor, watching her intensely. She closed her eyes. There was a dull pain in the centre of her forehead. She rested her face in the crook of her arm.

"Are you feeling down?" she heard him ask.

"I'm just tired," she lied, keeping her eyes closed.

She curled herself into a foetal position. Paradise was lost. He may never touch her or hold her again. That thought was unbearable.

"Here!" His voice spoke softly.

She opened her eyes. He was on his knees at her side. His eyes were full of light and his smile lit up the darkest corners of her mind. His hand was out-stretched. She moved instinctively. She held out her hand and he pulled her into his arms. They kissed slowly. She felt herself falling.

He was all over her, unbuttoning her blouse, loosening her skirt, easing down her tights. In moments they were naked. He kissed her stomach and caressed her thighs. She sucked his fingers, ran her hands along his back and wrapped her legs around him, all the time pulling him closer. Her whole body was set alight. A blazing passion seized her, raw, all-consuming, wild. She watched him moving above her, eyes closed, every sinew taut, straining for release. It may have lasted minutes but to her it seemed like hours. It was an altered state, the most natural drug in the entire universe. He moaned and rested his head on her stomach. She stroked his hair. They lay on the soft rug, their bodies aglow with the warmth of the fire.

His eyes moved all over her. There was no going back now. Logic and reason had been thrown to the winds. There was no use fighting the depth of that feeling. He stroked her feet. They both lay there resting. The music played on.

"This is paradise," she said.

"You can't get enough of a good thing, Marion." He smiled, then slapped her gently on the leg. "What about some live music? It'd be a good idea to hit town for a while. Then we can take up where we've left off."

He helped her dress. "You never see this part in the movies," he laughed. "I'll never know how you manage to get into those things." He held up her tights. Her world sparkled and fizzed, dazzled and soared, all in rich vibrant colours.

He chose Coleman's. It was jam-packed. They sat on two stools by the bar.

"Sex is all in the brain," he said. "The body is just the vehicle. Unless the mind is right, the experience can't be good."

She sat there gazing at him. She still felt awkward discussing sex with Peter. This was all so new.

"Sex can be the ultimate form of communication. There are times when two people can melt together. There's a merging, a chemical fusion. You can lose awareness of which hand belongs to you, whether that leg is hers or yours. You can hear the ebb and flow of the sea, feel the warm Sahara sands brush across your face, see the shooting stars fall to earth. For an infinitesimal moment two people can feel they are one. That's rare." He was in dazzling form. She listened. He lowered and softened his voice.

"It's all new to you. There's a long way to go. These are your first experiences." He took a long drink, then licked his lips. "Sometimes I can understand why people have sex with strangers. Then it's utter selfishness. It's never been my way. I like real connections, real people. But it's much harder when you're emotionally involved, when the other person really matters, when you really like her a lot. Then you have responsibilities. Then you want it to be a good experience, not just for yourself but for both of you."

116

She nodded in agreement. For her it was spiritual as much as sexual. She knew he'd probably laugh, but he was saying the same thing, only with different words. They had never spoken the same language. That had always been a problem. There was no one else she had ever wanted. There was only Peter.

It was after twelve by the time they got back to his flat.

"There's something I meant to show you." He called to her from the kitchen. "I'm just making coffee. I'll be there in a minute!"

Marion lay back on the sofa, exhausted.

She heard him turning on the TV and VCR. During the week he'd taped a documentary on megalithic monuments: massive stones and mounds, sculpted by the weather of centuries, flashed across the screen. There were dolmens, passage graves, portal tombs, standing stones and stone circles, each shaping and enhancing the Irish countryside, especially the tombs of Co. Meath. Then there it was: Newgrange, perched on its green throne, gazing down on the Boyne, untouched by the passing millennia, older than the pyramids of Egypt, the finest of all Europe's stone-age monuments.

Even Newgrange couldn't keep her awake. She fell into a soft slumber. The next thing she remembered he was pulling her towards him, his arm around her waist.

"Hey, it's time for bed. It's been a long day."

He picked her up in his arms and carried her to the bed. She lay there. He undressed her. The sheets smelt clean and fresh. She heard him in the bathroom. He put out the light and jumped in beside her. He pulled her legs over his and she lay in his lap while he kissed her. He brushed the hair away from her face. She placed her fingers on his lips and he licked them. They made love and slept. They woke and made love. She clung to him with her arm across his stomach. He stroked her and kissed her. She was swallowed in a wet mist of sensation.

At the breakfast table the walls had reformed.

"I'm going to visit the folks today," he declared. "Then I'll take it easy tonight. Another bit of space is required. Anyway, I couldn't keep this pace up for long. I'm wrecked."

He was separate again, a million miles out of reach. The colours turned pale and lost their sparkle. Without him there was a knawing and an emptiness. It had to be endured. He gave her the Newgrange tape to watch, on her own.

"See you!" he smiled weakly, standing in the open doorway.

"See you soon," she said.

She turned into the chilly morning air, a heaviness enveloping her. She wondered how he could let her walk away. There must have been a world of difference in what they each felt. For him, there wasn't the same need that gripped her, heart and soul. Why was there so much pain in the aftermath of all that pleasure? She walked home alone, lay on her bed, and wept.

CHAPTER 11

8.25. Just thirty minutes to go. The countdown was on. She looked again towards the mound. She remembered the first time she'd seen it: an afternoon in October. She had gone with Jim on a guided tour of the Boyne Valley. They'd visited Tara in the morning and then had lunch in Trim. She'd been amazed when they'd arrived at Newgrange. It seemed so intact, she'd thought then, all white and lustrous. She'd expected a broken down ruin after five-thousand-years. But it was fitting that Newgrange had been raised to its former glory.

She'd forgotten the framed photo she'd given Peter when he'd moved into his Terenure flat. It depicted the Winter Solstice. The golden light was streaming in through the roof-box. The whole passage was translucent. It symbolised the light of hope. She'd thought it might raise his spirits after he'd split with Jean. He'd hung it in his bedroom. It had witnessed their moments of rapture and their nights of anguish...

That phase had lasted just three months. They met once or twice most weeks. They hung out in pubs, went to talks, a few films and for the odd walk. Sometimes they stayed at his place, sometimes at hers. Wherever they ended up, there was always music playing somewhere in the background. She remembered that time in graphic detail. Nights he'd take her by the hand and lead her to the bedroom, tenderly kissing her breasts, stroking her hair, exploring every part of her. Nights when he tried to make love, becoming angry and moody, cursing the drink, rolling over on his side, not allowing her to touch him. Nights when she fell asleep happy in his arms; nights when she lay awake, feeling empty and alone.

He'd blamed her once for putting him under pressure to perform. Nothing could have been further from the truth. She was happy when he held her and rubbed his face against her skin. Her physical needs were simple. His membership of the feminist movement might have to be revoked.

It was the age-old difference that surprised and fascinated her. Not only his strength, the urgency and the vigour, but the aura of male energy that permeated his being. She experienced herself on a completely new sphere. Soft and yielding, open and receptive, an ocean of feeling, a sea of sensation: pure female. The fusion of the two was erotica in motion.

She was secretly glad of other worlds that had no intersection with Peter. There was the natural healer of home and family where life was stable and all was calm. There were her friends: a weekend spent with Niamh in London, a mid-week trip to Amsterdam with Lynn, and her regular chats with Jim, Conor and Anto. Around this time she started night-classes in counselling. Her career was going nowhere. It was time to explore new pastures.

Peter's moodiness was sporadic and random. It worried her but she didn't know what to do about it. He wasn't much of a candidate for therapy. He believed in sorting out his own 'crap'. But she was so afraid of losing him. She often felt nervous ringing him. She was either greeted by the noonday sun or frozen stiff by stark, chill torrents. With Peter, there were only extremities.

"Ah! So you passed with flying colours? Well done! That's my girl!"

It was early March. She'd just received the results of a project she'd been working on. She'd phoned to tell him.

"I was in Clare again at the weekend. We did some touring: the Burren, the Aillwee Caves and Lisdoonvarna. Great pubs! I met Jean last night. She's just spent a week in Achill. It sounds fantastic. I'm thinking of going there for a long weekend myself. Maybe next week."

She held her breath. Dare she even ask if she could go with him? Or horror of horrors, had he planned to go with Jean? She tried to sound casual, calm, in control.

"I'd love to see Achill. There's an ancient stone circle that Jim visited last year. He said the scenery was amazing."

She waited with her eyes closed. He hesitated.

"Well, you could come along if you'd like. I'll be doing plenty of walking though so you'll have to get fit pretty quick!"

Her heart danced with delight. She jigged from one foot to the other. She could hardly contain herself.

"I'd love to go! We've never been away together. I've a few days holidays left so there's no problem getting off work. Friday morning is fine. And I can take the Monday off too. I can't wait."

It was a beautiful spring morning, sunny and clear. Staring out through the window she could see fields covered with yellow daffodils and pure, white snowdrops, bright, green leaves budding on dappled trees, tiny birds singing a song of new life. She was more excited than she could ever remember. It had been a four-hour journey: Dublin to Westport by train, then to Achill Sound by bus. They'd booked a bed and breakfast over-looking the Atlantic. When they arrived there was only one room with two singles left. They hadn't much choice but to book in and bear it. They dropped off their things, had a quick shower and then went exploring.

They walked the length of the village, sussing out restaurants and pubs. They stopped off for dinner. Then the search started in earnest for live traditional music.

One place had a big open fire. That was the spot they chose. Marion had changed into her turquoise, silk blouse. She wore it with her black waistcoat and ski pants. She felt desirable, sensual. A few men at the bar kept eyeing her up.

"They're all gaping at you," he gestured towards the bar. "They're certainly having a good look. You have the pick of the place tonight!"

She shrugged her shoulders.

"I've no interest in any of them. I suppose it's a free country and I can't stop them looking but I don't like it. I'm just happy to be here with you."

He gave her a faint smile.

"Your loyalty is charming but also dangerous. You trust people too much. As a matter of fact, you trust me too much and I don't deserve it."

He took a few sips of Guinness, then continued. "In many ways you remind me of myself, a much younger, better version that existed long before the rot set in. You dwell in a utopian world of knights on white chargers and beautiful maidens, where good always triumphs. You're like a balm in this tired, disillusioned world. You know, my greatest fear is that you'll be tarnished by my farcical existence".

She shook her head. She didn't like it when he got this morose.

He gestured again towards the bar.

"You know they're all dreaming of getting into bed with you, of undressing you and doing all kinds of carnal things to you. The way I used to fantasise, before we got together." He drank a few more mouthfulls and then lowered his voice. "By the way, I meant to apologise for the other night. I just got carried away. You obviously have the same effect on all the guys."

She blushed at the thought of the last night they'd been together. He'd turned her upside down and inside out. He had been a wild, untamed creature, rolling over her, towering above her. She liked it better when it was soft and gentle, when he kissed and stoked her, and they drifted slowly towards the cliff's edge: a momentary hurtling through space, then rapid descent. He was full of mystery. The cosmos was nothing compared to Peter.

It was after ten when the musicians arrived. By that stage Peter was in full flight. The Guinness had reached its mellow phase. The pub had filled up. Two Austrian guys joined their table. Within minutes they treated Peter like an old friend. Every so often they stole a look at Marion. She was full of life that evening, thoroughly enjoying the banter. Peter led the singing: *Ride on, A song for Ireland, The Auld Triangle.*

It was after two before they got to bed. Peter could hardly stand. She helped him undress. He was asleep before his head touched the pillow. She undressed and then sat for a moment, gazing at him. He was beautiful. She put her arms around him and hugged him. She touched his lips with her fingers. If ever there was a feeling of love then this was it. She covered him up, making sure he was warm, then climbed into the other bed. A good night's sleep is what they both needed.

She was awoken early the next morning by him pulling up the covers and slipping in beside her. He kissed her neck and held her tightly, calling her name. They made love. Within minutes he was asleep again, his arms encircling her. She would never understand him. She would never know him.

The Austrians were heading for The Valley at noon and offered them both a lift. The beaches were legendary and the hostel there had its own pub. The Austrians chose an indirect root. Peter persuaded them to do a tour of the island. They took the road to Ashleam, heading for the Atlantic drive. The scenery was spectacular. Miles and miles of restless deep, blue ocean and steep, towering cliffs. A few times they stopped to stretch their legs, to stare at the glittering waves and to breathe in the cool, exhilarating air. At Keel they broke the journey for food and drinks. They agreed to stay in the pub for an hour. Marion left them, to wander around the craft shops and stroll along the sandy beach. It was heavenly. The sea was calm. The sun was turning a ruddy-orange on the horizon. It helped to clear her head.

Emotionally she knew she was riding a roller coaster. She could see all the classic signs of depression in Peter: inconsistency in moods, feelings of dire emptiness and sadness, bouts of hopelessness and flashes of anger. Excessive drinking didn't help either. But she had no control over that, or anything else in Peter's life, for that matter. She just kept hoping blindly that it would all change. Some days she felt desperate, when he was insensitive or refused to meet her. Then she'd plan to extricate herself from his life. But she could never do it. He was everything. It would be like losing her own soul.

The black sheet of night covered the sky when they reached The Valley. This time there was a double bed. They showered and lay down for a rest. They had bought supplies in Keel so that evening they cooked a mouth-watering dinner in the communal kitchen. The Austrians joined them. Later in the bar they played darts and pool. A group of locals began strumming guitars and playing tin whistles. It was the signal for the natives to arrive and the bar filled up in minutes. It had never registered with Marion before but now, watching Peter smiling and chatting, lost in a sea of faces, she realised this was where he truly reached his peak. He loved meeting new people: singing, theorising, connecting with all and sundry, yet completely untouched and unfettered. He could share so much of himself with strangers. In fact, he often said he had a great love for people. But then he could easily walk away and never look back. It was closeness and intimacy that unhinged him.

After the last song, one of the musicians announced

they'd continue playing on the beach until sunrise. Peter was all on for it. Marion was falling asleep but agreed to go along for the experience. The Austrians went too. The sky was amazing. A trillion, sparkling diamonds laid out on black, satin cloth could not have held a candle to the awesome stars that bespeckled the heavens that night. The moon in all her glory stole the show, casting silver beams across the living, breathing sea. The sound of the sea and the music lulled her to sleep. It was his turn to prop her up on his shoulder and steer her towards home. Dawn streamed through the curtains as they curled up under the covers. Neither of them moved a muscle until well after noon.

The Austrian's woke them, banging loudly on their door.

"Peter! We leave after breakfast for Keem. Are you coming with us?"

Peter's head appeared over the covers. He looked wrecked. He rubbed his hands across his forehead.

"Thanks, Christian. Give us half an hour. We'll be ready then."

He got out of bed. "I'm getting too old for this kind of lifestyle."

"How absurd!" she thought. He had just turned thirty.

"A shower should help and a black coffee." He took a towel from his bag and headed for the bathroom.

It was another beautiful day. Marion hadn't time to dry her hair so she hoped the sun spilling in through the car window would do the job. She held the guidebook in her hands.

"Could we stop to see the megalithic tombs and the stone circle? They're along this road somewhere, on the South side of Slievemore. The tombs are aligned with the sun on the Winter Solstice, just like Newgrange."

The Austrians quizzed her on everything she knew about Newgrange. They said they'd love to visit sometime, for dawn on December twenty-first. She was not marvellous at remembering faces but she didn't think they were here this year.

They found the tombs and the stone circle high up on a ridge of land. It was mucky, clambering up the side of the hill but they made it. They could see the island for miles around: green fields, pure air and pristine energy. She loved it.

"A really spiritual place," she said.

"Spiritual as in God-like?" he laughed. "Or spiritual as in exciting the mind and the senses?"

He had brightened up a lot since midday. He could never let a chance slip to challenge her.

"Spiritual as in transcending and inspiring!"

She'd rather not talk, just soak up the atmosphere. It was difficult to enjoy the moment when you had to analyse every feeling, every impulse.

"Transcending what?" he laughed again. "Time and space? It's your perception of reality. It doesn't mean it is reality."

She thought for a moment. "It's what I feel," she replied. "It's my truth at this moment in time."

She wasn't trying to score points. She simply wished to express what she was feeling.

"But we all know too well that feelings are fickle," he said. "They can change from moment to moment. And who knows for sure anymore what is true?"

They passed the Deserted Village. It had been a small thriving community before the 1840s, but became deserted during the famine years as the occupants moved to the coast, fighting for survival.

"Everything changes", she thought. "There's no stopping the movement of life, through birth, towards maturity, and then to decay."

Without the feeling that she was connected to some

overall cosmic plan it would sometimes be difficult to continue. She secretly wondered if that was why Peter fell into such black bouts of despair. He had no God on his side.

Keem Bay was exquisite, surrounded by hills on three sides, peering out towards the Minaun Cliffs and Clare Island. The sea was green and the sand golden. She pulled off her shoes and socks and ran barefoot into the water. This was her home.

"She's lovely," she heard Heinrich whispering to Peter as she dried her feet with his towel.

"She is," he answered and then turned away.

She walked with Christian to the Amethyst mines just a little down the road. The other two were already walking ahead. She found traces of crystal among the rocks and dug out a small, shiny amethyst with her bare hands. She was thrilled. This would be her lucky stone.

It had been a wonderful day. Back in The Valley they made dinner and then retired to the bar, drinking and listening to music. They were all tired. Peter said he was going to bed. Marion went up with him. It was their last night on the island. He was eager to make love. She knew something wasn't right but she'd no idea what it was. He became irritable. He said they'd make love in the morning.

"I love you anyway," she said.

"Isn't that a foolish thing to say?" he lashed out.

Something snapped inside her. She couldn't hold back the tears. The dam burst and she sobbed and cried like a broken child. She couldn't believe anyone could be so cruel. He'd never loved her. She lay there, just wanting to die. He tried to put his arms around her, anything to stop her crying. But she couldn't stop. She didn't want him to touch her. If only there was somewhere she could go to get away from him. She never knew how but she must have fallen asleep with sheer exhaustion.

The next morning she awoke to find him with his arms around her.

"I'm sorry, Marion, that I hurt your feelings. I'm sorry."

He hugged her and kept repeating the words. She felt numb and sick inside. There had been such an overload of pain that the fuse had simply blown. He was aroused again and wanting her. She pulled herself away from him and curled up into a ball, dragging the clothes over her body so he couldn't touch her. He sat staring at her.

"Okay, I'll go," he said. "Are you all right?" He looked ashen white.

She nodded, feeling as though she'd never be right again.

"I'm going out for a while. We need a break."

She'd never know how she got through that day. She walked alone along the beach, wandering where he was and what he was thinking. The fear of what would happen next was choking her. The only thing she was certain of was that they couldn't continue like this. Around twelve she went back to the room. He was there, packing. They hardly spoke. Both of them looked sick and scared. They walked to the bus station. They sat side by side on the bus and again on the long train journey back to Dublin. She tried to talk to him. He was mute. He just kept saying, "Now can you see why I need to be alone?" They shared a taxi to Rathmines.

"See you," he said.

"Bye," she whispered.

She couldn't put the key in the lock of the front door because her eyes wouldn't stop streaming. She went into the bathroom and took three Panadol, then crawled into bed and prayed for sleep to kill the pain.

A week later she rang him. There had been no word from him. She had been partially healed by her friend's kind words and their concern. He still sounded in desperate form.

"I can't see you again, Marion. We'll have to leave it. There's no use discussing it. It was a mistake. You'll have to accept it. I'm really busy here now. I have to go."

She nearly collapsed with the panic and dread.

"You can't just finish it like that." She was nearly crying. "I really need to see you. I've never asked you for anything before. I just need to talk to you. I could meet you after work, even just for a few minutes."

He hesitated. She persisted.

"Okay. It won't do any good, but if you need to talk that badly I'll meet you."

They met in Bewley's. It had been the beginning of many a night on the town in their past. He was already there. He looked haggard.

"I have to be alone, Marion. I'm trying to pull myself out of a huge, black hole. I'm at the bottom of a pit and I don't know when I'll get out of it. I need all the strength I've got. I can't love or be with anyone. You know how bad the other night was. I've made a decision. I'll never become involved with anyone again."

He didn't want to be there. He didn't want to see any more of her pain.

"I really like you. I thought it would work for us but it can't. You want someone who'll love and cherish you. I haven't got that in me. I have to be responsible for both of us and stop it now. I didn't want to put us through this. It can't change anything." He picked up the black, bitter mug of coffee and drank it straight down.

She knew it didn't matter what she said. Life without him was inevitable. She swallowed hard. She hoped she wouldn't start crying. There'd be plenty of time for tears, later.

"Why can't we still be friends?" She tried to cling onto any last strand.

"That doesn't work. I won't be seeing Jean again either. I'm just trying to survive, Marion."

She didn't understand any of it. She felt sick and weak. She was afraid she was going to faint.

"Years ago, before I ever met Jean, I went through the same kind of depression. I was suicidal. I didn't succeed in killing myself. I know when I'm going in over my head. I'm sinking and I have to be alone to have any chance of floating."

He saw the anguish on her face.

"There won't be anything like that. And you won't do anything foolish yourself? You won't run under a truck or anything?" He tried to make a joke of it.

"No. I'm the psychologist, remember?" She tried to sound calm. Inside she was collapsing.

"Maybe someday we'll meet again, when I've sorted myself out and we have a chance of making it. At the moment the only thing I can do is steer well clear of relationships. This isn't your problem. I know you're hurt by all this but I've got to go it alone." He drank the last mouthful of coffee. He kept his eyes diverted from her. He couldn't bear to see the devastating effect of his handiwork.

"We might as well go." He stood up. "There's no use talking or trying to understand. You'll just have to accept it."

She got up and put on her coat. There was a tightness across her chest. She found it hard to breathe. They walked out together. They stood on Grafton Street.

"I'm going this way," he said.

"Goodbye," she said and looked for one last time into his eyes. He never answered.

"Goodbye," she said again, but his eyes were cast downwards. He waved, walked away and was lost in the crowd.

There are different degrees of emotional pain. She knew this, in the same way that there are different degrees of physical burns. It wasn't necessarily the source of the pain, but the value you placed on the loss, on the disintegration of your dreams. Her pain that night had been third degree: shock, disbelief, nervousness, a sickness, an aching, a kind of death. She locked away everything he'd ever given her in her bottom drawer. She cried for hours, then had a bath and rang Niamh. She needed a friend. She was thankful she didn't have to spend the night alone.

The next two months were a kind of haze. She pulled herself out of the doldrums. Some days were fine; she'd laugh and get on with the job of living. It was when she heard a favourite song, or thought she'd caught a glimpse of him in the street, that her heart began pounding and her body perspired. At work, when she heard the phone ringing it never ceased to cross her mind that it might be him. She had lost a friend and a lover in one fell swoop. She missed him with all of her being. It was ironic that at last she understood how he must have felt in losing Jean. Her dreams at night were full of him. There were times she'd catch herself in the middle of a daydream. He'd be touching her, loving her. Sitting in the darkness of a cinema, walking through the busiest streets: nowhere was immune to the onslaught of his memory.

Niamh encouraged her to take a week's holiday in Marbella. They did plenty of sightseeing, even visiting the Alhambra in Granada. Peter would have been fascinated by the architecture, the way the natural light poured in through a series of holes cut into the wrought iron, making crazy patterns on the white marble floor. She'd never understand why he left her. She could never have left him, despite all the pain.

Lynn greeted her on her first morning back at work.

"Marion, you look great. All bronzed like a Spaniard!"

Lynn kept looking at her, obviously ill at ease. There must have been something on her mind.

"There was a call for you last Thursday," she finally said. "It was Peter."

Marion turned ashen white, all the sun's tan drained from her face.

"He just asked how you were and said if you wanted to you could give him a call."

Was she dreaming? She almost jumped out of her skin with sheer delight. He must have changed his mind. He might even want to live with her now. He had found himself again. Everything would be just fine.

She dialled the number with trembling fingers.

"Hello," she said tentatively.

"Well, hello there!" he sounded delighted. "Long time no hear. How are you?"

Her heart melted at the sound of his voice. "Okay. And you?" She tried to keep her voice from shaking.

"Up and down, but better than the last time we spoke. I've spent a lot of time clearing out the clutter, meeting new people, walking miles around the West and just getting on with living. I've still a long way to go, but I'm getting there."

They talked about music, books and films. It was the same as ever. He said he'd call her in a few weeks and they could meet for coffee. She had to be satisfied with that. It was better than nothing.

Three weeks later he rang. She had been feverishly awaiting his call. They agreed to meet in the Kylemore. She was a bundle of nerves. She wondered what he felt. She ordered coffee. Then he arrived. He was dressed in his casual gear. All the months of pain were forgotten in the twinkling of an eye. She still loved him.

"You're looking in good shape," he laughed.

"You look fine too!" She could hardly contain herself. They caught up on the previous three months. He'd written a dozen poems since he'd last seen her. He pulled a bundle of pages out of his jacket. She glanced through them. They spoke of his pain and his bewilderment.

"I was hurt," he said. "I abused your friendship. I'm sorry. I moved too quickly while I was still at a kind of mourning stage. I had been lacerated and I really had nothing left to offer you. I never wanted to hurt you. You're one of the nicest people I've ever met, Marion."

He paused to sip his coffee. He kept staring at her, tracing every minute change in her expression, wondering what all his messing had done to her.

"Emotionally I was a wreck. Well, let's face it, I've been divorced twice in the last six months! I need to watch every step I make. I don't want to turn into the kind of jerk I abhor."

He had written of his blackness, of his betrayal of her friendship, of his love for Jean, of his struggle to pick up the pieces and to live without both of them. Still Jean, Jean, Jean. Even when he was no longer with her she held an invisible power over him, like a ghost, haunting, stalking. Marion coolly shrugged her shoulders. In time he'd heal. Doesn't everyone?

"I'd like us to be friends again," he said.

Her face fell. She wanted him to hold her and to kiss her. She knew what he meant by friendship: nothing physical. She'd accept anything.

"I never wanted us to lose contact," he said, looking deep into her eyes, "but I just couldn't see any other way back then. Things are a little brighter now. The one-to-one thing just didn't work. Don't ask me why. It brought up too many feelings. It's easier this way. There are still lots of things we can do together."

It was just so good to see him, to spend even one moment with him. She felt like the condemned prisoner

133

who has just received a last minute reprieve.

They went their separate ways that evening. She was content that at least the ice had been broken.

The round of gigs, discussions and tours of Dublin recommenced. It was like old times. About five weeks it lasted. The cardinal error was for them to be alone. His mind had made a decision and he trusted its reliability. He'd forgotten to consult his body, heart and soul.

It was a Wednesday evening. He invited her back to listen to his new Bowie album. He lay on the floor, sipping wine and eating pizza. She joined him by the fire. It was past midnight. Every one of her senses was alert and alive, straining to move closer as he lay beside her.

"Are you ready for bed?" His eyes travelled slowly along the curves of her body.

"Yes," she said, not daring to breathe.

"You know there's only one bed," he smiled.

She opened her eyes and whispered, "Hold me!"

His eyes were black diamonds in the firelight, every facet ablaze with desire. "Are you in danger of falling?" he asked.

He reached towards her. They clung to each other, touching with a kind of desperation. They kissed long and hard. The blood throttled through her veins, pumping ferociously. She felt her loins about to burst. It was a feverish need to be all consumed.

He pulled her up by the hand. "Come on!" he whispered. "To bed."

The old ways refused to be banished. He was wild for the feel of her skin, the taste of her mouth, the sound of her moans, the smell of her. The onslaught of memory and desire was total. In the cold light of morning it was mere folly to deny the truth.

CHAPTER 12

Marion took a deep breath, to fill her lungs and to clear her head. The air was cold and dry. A short, sharp shock to bring her back to the moment was now what she needed. That was all many moons ago. Still, the pictures were crystal-clear; the wounds were wide and deep...

Somehow she'd lost track of the partings and the reunions after that night. There were at least four similar episodes. It wasn't working and he needed space; his withdrawal for weeks at a time; his reappearance and a new declaration of friendship. The inevitable nights spent feverishly glued together in bed. A comedy for some but a tragedy for her. Last Christmas he had been with her again and had even come to Newgrange. She remembered making love with him that night, wild, exciting, passionate. It had probably been the best experience of all.

The last night they were together they'd also made love. She hadn't seen him for two weeks. The writing had been on the wall but she had soldiered on, never having the courage to walk away. They'd met after work. He'd had a few drinks. Their talk flowed effortlessly. They spoke of films and books, work and friends. He was more anxious than usual to get back to her place.

When they arrived at her flat, he wanted her, desperately. Afterwards, he'd jumped up and told her something was very wrong. He handed her a dressing gown and draped it around her shoulders. He sat there staring at her, looking scared, unhinged. He pulled on his clothes hurriedly, went to the bathroom and splashed water on his face.

"I feel like I'm losing my mind. I'm losing control. I'm splitting into little pieces. Like some druggie on a downer."

She was frightened. She tried to reach him. "What is it Peter? What's wrong?"

He looked down at her as she sat on the bed.

"Don't lay that psychology stuff on me." He was sad, confused and angry. "I have to leave. I'm damaged. I'm dangerous. You deserve much more than this. I can't put us through this any longer."

She felt the panic rising in her gut. "Don't go!" she pleaded.

"I have to, Marion." He pulled on his jacket.

She felt like screaming. "How can you do this to me? How can you walk away and leave me, like some stranger who doesn't mean a damn to you?" But she couldn't speak. Shock. Devastation. The door closed behind him. The walls tumbled in, leaving her gasping for air, choking, internally bleeding.

Two weeks later she'd rang him. He was harsh, cold and deadly serious.

"Let it go," he'd said.

There was no point in arguing, in asking to meet him. They had been through all that before. "Goodbye!" she whispered, still thinking he'd ring her, sometime, somewhere.

"Bye," he said.

Neither rhyme nor reason: the end.

If she'd let them come the tears would flow and keep on flowing. Even here, with so many onlookers, she could so easily break down and cry bitter tears. It had been a dream that had turned to a nightmare. There had been many nights when she couldn't stop the deluge. Like the time she was headed for a party in Chapelizod and *Nights in white satin* came on the radio. She'd been embarrassed, but she couldn't stem the tide. She avoided all the old haunts. Her greatest fear was meeting him. In case he would pretend not to know her, in case he was with another woman, in case he would smile and it would start all over again.

She walked along the kerb. Her fingers trailed the fence. It was good to go through all of this. It was cleansing, healing. At last the morning had come. It had stood so often like a beacon in the darkness. Newgrange: her salvation. All of a sudden she stopped dead in her tracks. She had the strangest feeling she was being watched. She turned around quickly. A man in his mid-thirties was indeed looking at her, standing just a few yards away. He looked vaguely familiar. He had light brown hair and a small shapely beard. Everything else about him was blue: his eyes, his windcheater and his denims. He was obviously taken aback when she turned around so abruptly and caught him watching her. He smiled shyly and walked over.

"Hello. Cold isn't it?"

His voice was a little hoarse. He cleared his throat.

"It is," she answered cautiously.

"I remember seeing you here last year. You weren't in the chamber, though, as far as I recall."

She relaxed again. He had just remembered her from last year's vigil.

"Yes,", she replied. "I wasn't lucky enough to be in the cairn. But then no one actually got to see the sun. I'll be inside this morning, though. I really hope he'll make a big effort to fill every inch of the chamber with his golden rays. Some years I know he doesn't feel in the mood. Even so, it'll be a hugely significant event for me. And who knows, he might delight us all and drench us from head to toe in brilliant sunlight!"

He smiled, seemingly delighted by her description of the sun.

"Yes. It's still a bit cloudy to the east but there's a long way to go before the sun puts in an appearance. I was in the chamber last year and I didn't see anything. I have been there on one occasion in the past when the sun did honour us with his presence. It was spectacular. I'll never forget that dawn as long as I live. I hope you'll get the chance to see it this morning for yourself. Forgive me, I haven't even introduced myself. I'm Brendan Connolly."

"Hello Brendan, I'm Marion."

"Hi Marion!" he cleared his throat. "I remember you had a friend with you last year."

Marion visibly winced as the memory of last year's solstice sprang to mind. It was a morning just like this. She had been so giddy, running like a child against the wind, her long jagged scarf streaming out behind her, not satisfied until she had completed the full circumference of the mound. She felt self-conscious then, wondering if this guy had watched her while she sat on the steps, love and adoration streaming from her eyes as she gazed up at Peter.

"I'm sorry. I didn't mean to pry." A deep blush spread across his face and he cast his eyes downwards.

She knew then that he hadn't meant to hurt her. He was just making conversation. He was obviously quite a shy guy himself.

"It's ok," she feigned a smile. "I'm here on my own this morning. A lot can change in a year." She swallowed hard, trying to recover her composure. "Loss is the only certainty in life." She had to smile at the absurdity of quoting Peter on this one.

"I know the enormous changes that can happen in a year." He turned towards the cairn. "Both of my parents passed away in the past twelve months. I miss them a lot."

"Oh! I'm really sorry." She instantly connected with his grief. "That must have been so hard for you."

He nodded, keeping his gaze fixed on the cairn as he spoke.

"We were always a close family. I'm the only son. I have one younger sister, Maeve. My father wasn't sick or anything. He was eighty years old. It was just old age."

Marion could see the tears welling up in his eyes. She wanted to comfort him. "You must have been good friends," she said.

"You are so right." He gave her a weak smile. "We were more like best buddies than father and son. His mind was so rich and sharp. We'd sit for days and nights discussing local history, and it's many a talk we had on the origins of Newgrange. It was he who first sparked my love for castles, ruins and the like. As a boy of six or seven he'd bring me on tours around Meath. It was a perfect county to be reared in. We followed the football every Sunday afternoon in the summer, supporting the home county. It was a great childhood. I can still vividly remember the picnics at the mouth of the Boyne, the twice-yearly excursions to Dublin, and the smell of home cooking wafting from the kitchen when I'd come home after school."

Marion stood there, watching him intensely. She could sense his embarrassment. He was obviously not used to airing his feelings in public. She wanted to reach out to him, to say something that might lessen his pain.

"You have great memories of your lives together. That may increase the pain in the short-term because you miss them both so much, but you will always know that they loved you and that is a very rare gift. To love and to be loved, for me, is the ultimate human experience."

"Yes," he almost whispered. "For me, too."

Their eyes met and they both smiled.

Marion felt he needed to talk more about his parents.

"Your Dad sounds like a lovely person," she said.

"Oh, he was inspirational. I learned so much from him. Even when his eyesight began to fail and he couldn't read very well, he'd listen to audio tapes and to the radio. And of course I travelled home as often as I could. He knew everything that was happening in the world. He had a brilliant mind and a kind word for everyone. He died last January from a heart attack. The last memory I have of him was when I was leaving for Dublin. He hugged me and said, 'Take care, Brendan, we'll talk again soon.' I never saw him again."

He paused to catch his breath. His voice was shaking. Marion sensed that he needed to face these scalding memories, to speak the truth of his heartfelt loss. Newgrange was the altar where he had chosen to lay down his burden.

"It was a terrible shock for all of us," he continued to unburden his soul. "My mother was naturally devastated. They had loved each other so much. We couldn't do enough to keep her with us. She died in August. She was a little over seventy. I know she died from a broken heart."

His voice was full of emotion.

"Sorry, Marion. I never meant to say all this. It's just that you're so lovely to talk to and it's not every day that I find myself at Newgrange on the solstice!"

Marion stood close beside him. She was deeply touched that he had chosen to share the core of his suffering with her.

"You've had a desperate year. I can only imagine the pain you must have felt."

She wanted to reach out to him in some way. She had lost the man she loved and that had caused her great pain. Still, the thought of losing any member of her family filled her with an even greater dread. To lose someone who has supported and loved you throughout your life would be unbearable. Yet, she knew that others had survived even the most appalling tragedies. The capacity of the human spirit to rise above such anguish and to overcome the greatest deprivation was limitless. But it was nevertheless a long and lonely road.

He recovered his balance and managed a dim smile. "This is the best place to be," he said, "for anyone who has experienced any kind of pain or loss. Newgrange, built as a mausoleum for the select few, perhaps for a dynasty of kings or spiritual leaders. To me, Newgrange has always been a symbol of life more so than death. A reminder that even on the darkest day there is the chance of rebirth, the chance of new life. I really wanted to be here this year, to remember and to celebrate the lives, not the deaths, of my parents. This is what I feel Newgrange represented to the ancient people who built her: the mansion of everlasting life."

She could feel a tingling sensation shoot up along her spine. Brendan was certainly a man on her wavelength.

"It's a lovely thought", she smiled, "the idea of Newgrange as a temple of rebirth. I agree wholeheartedly. Why else would these ancient people have built such a fantastic solar centre?"

She could feel her excitement heighten, just like old times. "You said earlier you had been inside the chamber once before on the solstice. How come you have been so fortunate to get a second chance when there is a waiting list of many years?"

He laughed, a little embarrassed.

"I hate to admit it but I have some close friends in the inner sanctum who have issued me with a privileged pass. I work as an archaeologist. The first exposure I ever had to an archaeological dig was on this site. Imagine a kid of fifteen, hell-bent on discovering the mysteries of life, ablaze with speculation about the enigmatic mound that was just a few miles down the road. It was the last summer that work was ever done here. I was allowed to do some chores for the experts: making tea, carrying stones, it didn't matter what. It was a dream come true. I've worked on many sites around the world since then, but nothing compares to my passion for Newgrange."

Marion could hardly believe her luck. A real live archaeologist was standing less than two feet in front of her, chatting away, confiding in her, all on the site of Newgrange, just minutes before the Winter Solstice. He seemed kind and sensitive. It was just what she needed, a new friend to connect with.

"Tell me something about your work, Brendan. What does an archaeologist do?"

He gave her a boyish grin. "I probably love talking about my work too much! But I'll certainly tell you anything you'd like to know. First though, what do you do yourself?"

"I'm working with the John of God at the moment. After years of not knowing what I wanted to do I've finally discovered clinical psychology. I'm finding it fascinating."

He nodded. "Tough, I'm sure and challenging, but very worthwhile."

"Yes, it is. Now tell me all about the life of an archaeologist."

"Well, when most people hear the word archaeology they invariably think of excavations in distant exotic lands such as Egypt, Greece or Rome, the discovery of Tutankhamun's mask, or the Derrynaflan hoard containing such priceless beauties as the Ardagh chalice. When I was a kid I was no exception. I had visions of lost civilisations, unsolved mysteries, grinning skeletons and buried treasure. I'll never forget the day I started digging in our back garden, searching for a cache of jewels. After an hour of hard slogging I was getting tired. I hadn't found a thing. This was no fun. I threw another sod of earth onto the growing pile to my left. I suddenly saw something gleaming. I pounced on it. It was filthy but there was no doubt that it was a ring. I couldn't believe it. I washed it in soap and warm water. It was still intact: a gold ring with a tiny, aquamarine stone. I presented it proudly to my mother. I was hooked for life."

He stood there, grinning again. He was a lucky man indeed to love his work so much. That was clearly written all over his face. He certainly didn't fit Marion's idea of the eccentric, pith-helmeted professor, straining to decipher inscriptions on ancient tombs. He was actually quite attractive and very good company.

"I can imagine how exciting it is to go in search of lost cities and priceless artefacts," she said.

"Unfortunately the day to day reality is not always as glamorous or exciting," he shrugged. "Most sites are less spectacular than the golden tombs of the Pharaohs and are excavated on a far smaller scale, with little or no public acclaim. But each site is unique and must be treated with the utmost respect. Modern archaeology is a highly sophisticated scientific discipline. Most of the work concerns documentation of the site. When the excavation is over all that remains are the records that have been compiled. A vital part of the work is, of course, trying to interpret the whole site and reconstructing the lifestyle, the beliefs and the culture of the people who once inhabited the area. That's a highly responsible job and it's really the crux of the whole work."

He dragged a hand through his hair and then plunged both hands deep inside his pockets.

"I could go on forever like this", he laughed. "It's my hobby horse. Do tell me if I'm getting too technical or going off on a tangent."

"It's fascinating," Marion declared. "I've always wondered what was involved in a dig. Please do continue."

"Okay!" His face positively glowed as he spoke. "I've been involved in several digs as a field worker, mainly in the South of England, and I've done my fair share of piecing together records after the excavation, in Dublin, New York, London, and a few other locations around the world. This can take twice as long as the excavation. Incredible, isn't it? Some objects need to be repaired or reconstructed. Most of Newgrange was such a site. You can imagine how long it took to sort out the many layers and artifacts on this site?"

She nodded. It seemed to be a truly huge undertaking. He was speaking again.

"Another very important part of the work involves dating the objects. Basic chemical analysis can be used on ceramic items, such as pottery. On organic items, radiocarbon dating is fantastic because it's not confined to a particular region…"

Marion's mind drifted to Peter. He'd really love this, having the chance to update his knowledge and to interrogate an expert. But Peter was no longer part of her life. Brendan had stopped speaking and was staring at her again.

"Where did you originally study archaeology?" she asked, curious to find out more about the man, not just the archaeologist.

"In Oxford. I wanted to study in Dublin but the right type of course wasn't available. My County Meath influence meant that I desperately wanted to specialise in prehistoric archaeology. The portion of history that extends back before the time of written documents and archives had captured me hook, line and sinker. I still enjoy the practical work, though mostly these days I lecture in Trinity and I'm involved in projects with the National Archives and the Museum."

"That's amazing!" she shook her head. "I just started studying clinical psychology in Trinity last September."

"Incredible! It's a small world, Marion. Maybe we'll see each other around campus then." He looked really pleased.

"I hope so," she was delighted too. She began to

wonder then about his private life. He wasn't wearing a ring. She was just curious. The last thing on her mind was a relationship. She just felt a kind of pull towards this guy. Besides that, she had to concentrate on licking her own wounds dry before she'd ever be ready to become involved again. She wouldn't make the same mistake as Peter and mess up another person's life. She had learned that lesson the hard way.

"What was Oxford like?" she asked.

"I really enjoyed myself there. I met some great people from all over the world." He sighed, then feigned a smile. "That's where I met Terri. She was my girlfriend for years and years. But everything passes. That's the way of life. If everything remained static then I'd be out of a job. And if no one ever loved and lost then you'd be out of a job too!"

"That's true enough," she smiled.

"I'm often asked how archaeology differs from history."

He changed the subject rapidly, obviously not wanting to dwell on memories of his relationship for too long.

"Well, history is the study of the past using documents and inscriptions, whereas archaeology uses objects and other excavated evidence as the main source of data..."

She found herself tuning out. How many other people had experienced this kind of pain? Brendan had lived through it. But how had it affected his life? How had it changed him? This is what she'd love to ask. She needed reassurance that she'd be okay, that in time she could remember Peter's smile without bleeding inside.

"...Archaeologists seek to satisfy the individual's curiosity about the past, about their forefathers." He was still speaking. "People have speculated about human origins and the remote beginnings of life for centuries. Everyday millions of people file past museum displays.

Reconstructing the past is a huge tourist industry. There's this inbuilt need to know where we've come from, to discover where we're going. And this brings us full circle to Newgrange."

He glanced at his watch. "8.35. Time is ticking away. Exciting isn't it?"

They both turned their gaze towards the cairn. The whole sky had brightened and was now a hazy blue. Surely dawn couldn't be postponed much longer. The grey weather-beaten stones gazed back, with sunken eyes that had seen five-thousand-years of sunrises and sunsets. She felt the excitement gathering, somewhere low down in her belly. She had shed a lot of excess baggage already this morning. She felt lighter. The dawning of a new life was but moments away. She was glad now that there would be someone to share it with. Brendan would be there too.

"It was once believed that the high kings of Tara were buried at Newgrange." He turned to look at her again. "There was a reference to it in an early twelfth century book, called *Senchas na relec*. Newgrange actually predates Tara by three thousand years. It's a nice story but it has no basis in fact."

"Tara is beautiful," she interrupted. "It's one of my favourite places."

"It's a very special place, that's for sure."

She suddenly noticed his deep, blue eyes sparkling in the gathering light; kind eyes, full of soul.

"On the evening of the Summer Solstice," he continued, "hundreds still gather on Tara hill. I often just go and sit there. It still retains an air of romance and mystery."

He must be a bit of a dreamer, an idealist too, she figured.

"You seem to be really into all of this yourself?" He had turned to look at her again. "I can see these places mean a lot to you."

"Yes, I love the feel of ancient sacred places." She smiled up at him, realising that she was enjoying his company immensely. "I've been to Tara once. It was last August, on a warm, clear evening. It was a lovely experience to stand there and dream of all that had gone before. I'd love to go there for the Summer Solstice, maybe next year."

"It's a great place. You'll have to go back there again. I live just down the road from Tara. I can see the hill from my bedroom. I'll show you around some time– the hill I mean–if you like, Marion?"

She broke into a wide smile, delighted. "I'd love that, Brendan. And now getting back to Newgrange, what does archaeology tell us about the people who built her?"

He clapped his hands and blew on his fingers. The chill was taking hold, seeping in. But he was still enraptured.

"They were a hunting and farming community…"

Her mind trailed off again. She couldn't help comparing him to Peter. Last year he'd stood on this same site, telling her about the early farmers who had built Newgrange. He hadn't been far out in his hypothesis. "Told you so!" She could hear his words calling to her through the miles and the unbridgeable space that now separated them. She wondered where he was and what he was doing. He must have remembered that this morning was the long awaited solstice when she'd be admitted to the chamber. Surely he couldn't have forgotten. She felt a stab of pain in her gut. She'd stick to this moment.

Brendan's mellow voice was speaking again.

"It's thought that the cremated remains of the dead were placed in the bowls in the chamber. We'll see them this morning. There's one in each of the three areas in the chamber. Pottery items such as food vessels and metal objects, jewellery and weapons would often have been buried with the dead. Attractive coloured stone beads, mace heads and round balls have also been found in many tombs. If you like to see some of the stone objects that have been excavated at Newgrange they're on display in the National Museum. These must have possessed great symbolic significance for the ancient community. Beautiful stones seem to have held a fascination for people since earliest times and were traded over long distances to be made into jewellery and amulets. We've always been suckers for beauty."

She was aware that he was looking at her again, taking in every detail. She felt a little uneasy but she was also pleased to be getting so much attention.

"I love reading the old legends of Newgrange," she said, "especially the stories of Aonghus and the Dagda."

"The Dagda was the pre-Celtic sun-God, as far as I remember."

Marion couldn't recall the last time she'd felt so attracted to anyone. She tried to keep her mind focused on what he was actually saying.

"He was probably the equivalent of Ra, the Egyptian sun-God. The Egyptians believed that both Ra and Osiris had the power to resurrect the dead. I've spent a few months doing research in Giza. The Great Pyramid there is absolutely enormous and must have taken generations to build. The same is believed to have been the case with Newgrange. It's estimated to have taken three generations to carry the stones from the nearby quarry, to transport the huge boulders probably from Wicklow by log-boat and then across land. It was an amazing feat of engineering but, above all, of cooperation. Egypt built its wonders by enslaving thousands, perhaps millions of unfortunate souls, forcing them to toil in the boiling hot sun, to build a mausoleum for some vengeful Pharaoh. The construction of Newgrange has no such legacy. I like to think it was built by the ordinary people of the Boyne to celebrate their faith and belief in everlasting life. Though its builders have long since returned to the great

Dagda in the sky, their astounding creation remains. Not a bad way to mark your earthly existence!"

Marion was spellbound. It was like stumbling over a polished diamond on the roadside when you least expected it. What a lovely surprise!

"I've read bits and pieces about the Neolithic age but it's hard to bring it to life from a book," she replied. "But when you talk about it, it begins to take on colour and depth. I find it impossible to remember all those dates and details, but when I close my eyes I can feel it all. I can see the ancient people travelling in long boats along the Boyne, trudging through fields, waiting in the cold and the dark, united in their belief, expectation and adoration. People have probably not changed that much over the last five-thousand-years. We still struggle to make sense of this life. We still risk everything to feel loved. There is always the inevitable pain of loss and there is forever the hope of happiness. That's what Newgrange means to me: a shrine of hope."

He nodded. "For me too, that's why I'm here today. It's not just an interesting monument. People have prayed here, wept here and probably made their vows here for millennia. We are just following in their footsteps. It brings..."

He broke off in mid-sentence. He had caught sight of someone.

"Maybe it's his girlfriend?" Marion shrugged and prepared to disentangle herself. She was getting used to disconnecting in mid-stream.

"I'm sorry, Marion. I've just spotted my friend, Thomas, in the crowd. He's an annual pilgrim here. He's quite an amazing character. He's into the whole spiritual area. He's a healer, among other things. I first met him around the time Terri and I split up. I was in bits. I'd never thought very deeply about spirituality before then. I'd been reared with the standard religion but that never held much interest for me. I felt some amazing things when I went to him for healing. He moved his hands over me but there was no touch involved. Weird stuff! He was a maths teacher for years before he discovered healing. I guess it can take a long time for any of us to find our path in life. He's been a great help to me too since my parents passed over. It'd be hard to survive if I didn't believe that I'll meet them again someday. I'll just go over and have a word with him. I'll invite him over, if you like. He's fascinating to talk to. He has some stimulating theories on Newgrange, too."

"Sure. I'd like to meet him."

Marion relaxed again. He had just spotted his friend–a healer. He might be interesting to meet.

Brendan gave her a boyish grin.

"I'll be back in a few minutes, ok?" He took a long look at her, in case she'd suddenly vanish, and then hurried off in search of the healer.

CHAPTER 13

Marion glanced towards the gate. She was surprised at the number of people who had gathered there: perhaps seventy, maybe more. She spotted the pre-Raphaelite girls who were still chatting with the tall Germans. She'd never dreamt that a pilgrimage to Newgrange could turn into a social event. Her idea had been to experience the morning in solitude. She should have guessed that those who were compelled to come here must surely share some kind of common ground.

Time was ticking away. She might as well drift back again and fit the remaining jigsaw piece that was tightly clenched inside the deep recesses of her mind...

It was out of the blue that she'd met him. It was the previous month, in early November. She was walking under the Bank of Ireland pillars in Westmoreland Street on her way to meet her cousin, Mike. It was a busy Saturday afternoon. Her heart nearly burst when she saw him. She couldn't believe it. He looked just as startled but he recovered his composure in an instant. He was all smiles, all over her.

"Well hello there! It's been a while. How are you doing?"

"It must be nine months," she stumbled.

She wondered if this was another of those dreams. Only last week she'd dreamt that he'd been crucified. She was kneeling at the cross, watching him dripping with blood. He was dying. She was unable to do anything to save him. She'd awoken with a start, feverish and alone.

"I'm fine," she lied. She was glad her lips could move and her voice could speak. Habit, she supposed. She tried to look indifferent, in control, but she feared she wasn't doing a great job of it.

He kept looking at her, smiling, as though they were old buddies who had just happened to lose touch. The last memory she had of him was one of utter melodrama. Life was absurd! He certainly looked stable enough now. But anyway, his smile and his laughter had always disarmed her.

"Your hair has grown much longer," she said.

"Yeah, the ageing hippie! Yours has grown too," he gestured. "You're looking really good. Are you still working with that social group?"

"No. I finally made up my mind to do something more practical and to jump in at the deep end, not to spend my life getting bogged down in theory."

She placed her hand on the granite pillar to steady herself. She needed something solid to prop her up. She had just seen a ghost.

"Great. So you've changed jobs?" He was all enthusiasm.

"I started clinical psychology a few months ago." She was glad to report that something had changed. "I'm studying a few days each week in Trinity and then doing a few hours of practical work with St. John of God. I'd rather work with real people and real problems. I've become experienced at helping people to deal with their pain."

Dealing with her own pain was the problem, she thought. Talking to friends had helped and going for counselling. Then there were all the books she'd read: *Women who love too much; The dance of intimacy; The bonds of love*, to name but a few. She'd certainly gained some important insights into herself over the past nine months.

She had often rehearsed this meeting. The way she'd act so cool and offer nothing but a throwaway comment. "Thanks for all the heartache, Pal!" Or maybe she'd call out, "Hello Peter. Hope you have a good life! See you," and then walk briskly away, with her head held high. The reality was a different story, as it so often is.

"That's brilliant. It's good to hear you've found your niche. So it's going well?" He seemed genuinely pleased she'd found something fulfilling.

"So far I love it. It's tough at times but I enjoy connecting with people at a really deep level. I've always been a sucker for that. Professionally it seems to work fine." She didn't add that personally it had been a disaster, but he already had first-hand proof of that.

"So a lot has changed?" he asked.

"Yeah. It keeps on moving, doesn't it?" She wanted to sound all philosophical, the wise woman who had her life well sorted. "Life is a series of experiences. Some we relish and love to savour, whereas others we would never choose. But either way we have to get on with it."

"Life's a bitch, and then you die! Remember that old adage!" he laughed.

"And are reborn!" She couldn't resist it. God, how she missed him.

"Some things never change. No, I haven't been saved yet, God forbid!" He paused to take a good look at her. "Are you heading that way? I'll walk with you, if you don't mind. Or do you have an appointment? Have you time for a coffee? Bewley's is handy."

She still had thirty minutes before meeting Mike. Some part of her answered, "Sure!" She followed him into the coffee shop.

"You choose a seat and I'll get the coffee."

She sat down and watched him as he stood there in the queue. He was wearing faded denims, a navy shirt and a short black jacket. He looked lean and fit. She still loved him. She probably always would.

He returned with two mugs of white coffee.

"Still milk and no sugar?" He was smiling again.

"You've a good memory," she said.

To keep clear and cool was her goal. Her stomach churned and she felt hot flushes shoot all over her body. But it no longer mattered what she felt or what she wanted. All that lay buried in the past. She had to remain centred in herself.

"It's impossible to forget some things," he said softly.

He was watching her, taking in every detail, wondering what life was really like for her. She looked away.

"So have you been to any good gigs lately?" he asked.

Such good cheer! It must be one of his happy days or maybe he had changed dramatically.

"Yes. I've been to Whelan's a few times with the gang. I went to Loyko last week. They're brilliant."

She wanted to sound as though life was full and she was having a ball. She never mentioned that Lynn had gone to Australia to work for two years, and that Conor had met a girl and spent most of his time with her. She'd made a few new friends at Trinity, but overall she was lonely. The truth was she didn't want to tell him anything about her life. It would be too painful. He had walked out on her. He had rejected her life, her love, everything she stood for. She had tried to claw it all back. She was still struggling. He deserved nothing.

"I've gone to see them once. Great musicians."

He ran his fingers through his hair. She'd noticed this mannerism thousands of times before. If only it could have worked between them.

She glanced at the stained-glass window behind him. Harry Clarke's magnificent colours flooded their table. She remembered the day they'd gone to the Municipal gallery to view *The Eve of St. Agnes*. Then there was the church he'd brought her to in Terenure. It had been full of Clarke's work. She had marvelled at the huge domed window with its brilliant colours. He'd insisted though that it wasn't an original Clarke, it was a Clarke Studio window, and that somehow this was an enormous difference. Her gut twisted and she swallowed hard.

There was silence. They looked at each other. Different sides of her reacted in diverse ways to the sudden reappearance of Peter Kerrigan. One side had thrived on his friendship, on the sharing of his world, on his sense of fun and his glorious mind, on his loving fingers and the awakening of her sexual being, on his belief in her. This side yearned to experience more of him. Then there was the side that was red-raw, angry, feeling hurt and betrayed, always searching for an answer to why he hadn't loved her. A third side—survival—rejoiced when he'd gone, desiring only equilibrium, no further bouts of emotional upheaval. The sight of this dark stranger brought back the knowledge that her pain had reached dangerous proportions, and that her judgment and trust in herself had been irretrievably damaged. She was sure there were other sides. At the moment these were silent, awaiting a more opportune moment to emerge.

"I'm still working in Compex," he broke the silence.

She nodded. Yes, of course she'd love to know all about him but it was too sore to ask. It was better for him to think she no longer cared.

"I'm doing a lot more art work now. I'm working on another CD cover at the moment. *Renegade*, the group's called. It gives me something to do in the long, cold evenings. I still live alone," he added, searching her face for some reaction.

It was what she wanted to hear but she didn't give the slightest sign that it had registered. She wondered if he'd slept with anyone. Even the thought of it hurt her.

She hadn't even looked at another man. She had felt like a bride and a widow, all within a couple of months.

She took another drink of her coffee. There was no reason for him to have to live alone. She would have given him everything. But he'd chosen to cast her aside, like some useless piece of junk.

"I've moved flat though," he continued. "Now I'm in an apartment in James Street. I always loved the area. Ironic isn't it that I'm only living across from the brewery and it's the one time in my life–probably since infancy–that I've seriously cut down on the gargle. It was destroying me and anyone I was close to." He kept staring at her. "I'm staying at..."

She closed her ears to the address. The truth was that part of her screamed to be readmitted to his life. The rest of her knew it would cripple her.

"That's good," she tried to smile. "So you've got what you wanted."

More silence. Just the clink of coffee cups. He hadn't taken his eyes off her for a moment.

"And what about you? Still in Rathmines?" He tried to draw her out.

"Yes," she said. "We really had some great times in the early days." It was her voice, but she could hardly recognise it. She sounded cold and distant. "I'll never forget the fun we had, but it all ended rather abruptly."

"We had many good times, that's true." His black eyes smiled weakly. "I only wish there was some way of wiping out the murkier experiences. If only the good memories were all that remained."

He took another sip of coffee. Her eyes focused in on his fingers, those same fingers that had stroked her and held her. She would trade almost anything for the chance of being touched by him again. But she had to be strong here or all could be lost. Her red-bricked walls towered high above her. She realised in that moment how much she had changed. At last she was taking care of herself.

"But it was all part of reality. At least it was my perceived reality." She had to keep playing with words. There was nothing about suffocating pain, about the nights she'd cried herself to sleep.

"It was clinical depression," he said. "Now that's your department! Something was very wrong. I couldn't take the closeness. I'm a lot clearer now. I'm still living from day to day but it's becoming easier."

At last she had an explanation for all that pain. "You wouldn't have had to be a psychologist to figure that one out!" She tried to pass it over. Part of her wanted to sit here forever, holding onto his every word, the part that still grasped at straws. Her newly built protector demanded that she leave. She glanced at her watch.

"I've arranged to meet my cousin," she said. "I'd better be going."

Outside the afternoon was turning to dusk. The streets were floodlit. She could feel the wounds opening and the tears gathering, like menacing storm clouds. She still showed him detachment, indifference. He asked her where the best place would be to buy a curtain pole. It was all surreal, like some demented Dali painting. She had to get away in case he mentioned seeing her again. Would she be able to refuse, though accepting might well be the end of her?

"See you in another few years!" She wanted to make it clear: Don't call me!

"See you!" He smiled, waved, and was gone.

She walked through the crowds. Was there no end to this pain? How could love hurt this much?

That night when she was alone, the cool, in-control woman collapsed in a heap on her bed. The fragile, sobbing child was inconsolable.

CHAPTER 14

She spotted Brendan walking towards her with his friend. She took a deep breath. It was time to let go.

"Marion, this is my friend, Thomas. Thomas, meet Marion."

"Delighted to meet you, Marion!"

She shook his outstretched hand. He could have been any age between fifty and sixty. The bushy grey beard probably added a few extra years to his actual age. It was his eyes though that captivated her. They radiated wisdom, compassion and love. They were the eyes of a sage, yet the eyes of a child: clear, uncluttered, free.

"My old friends, Aisling and Ray, are over there by the gate," Brendan pointed. "I've promised to go back for a quick update on how they're doing. They got married on the Summer Solstice. Now they're expecting their first child. They've just asked me to be Godfather. I'll be back in a few minutes, okay?"

He tore himself away and walked back towards the gate. She could see him hugging his friends.

"He's a lovely guy," Thomas said.

"He seems really nice. We've only just met."

He smiled then nodded.

"Ah! but who knows what old forgotten links there are between two people, seemingly strangers. Sometimes we meet a person and there's a kind of recognition. You already know each other, intimately. You've already shared many lifetimes together. Some meetings don't happen by chance."

Yes, she'd had that experience with people before, with Jim, Niamh and unmistakably with Peter. The idea of past lives wasn't new. It would certainly explain why we're inexplicably drawn to some individuals.

"Brendan says you're a healer," she said.

"I channel spiritual healing. It's the oldest from of healing known and the most natural. We are all spirit beings, housed in bodies for our stay on earth. Sometimes we lose sight of who we are and get caught up with the trappings of life. Then we require healing. Spiritual healing is completely non-intrusive. Whatever healing the person needs is provided by spirit."

He paused, probably awaiting some reaction. She could imagine Peter standing beside her, cynical and critical. He would call it nonsense. To her, it made a lot of sense.

"It sounds fascinating. I'd like to try it sometime," she said.

"Certainly," he replied. "I have a small centre in Dublin. I must give you my card."

He handed her a small card with his details printed in gold on blue: *Thomas Cleary: Spiritual Healing and Meditation.*

"Brendan tells me you'll be in the chamber at dawn," he continued. "It's a wonderful experience. It's something that will stay with you always. I had the good fortune many years ago of witnessing the breath-taking spectacle. It marked the beginning of a new phase in my life. I feel it will be the same for you."

His eyes twinkled. His words filled her with a mixture of excitement and comfort. She felt a tingling, prickly sensation all over her body, as though she had just been connected to a giant, electric current.

"The light will not fail you today, Marion. You needn't worry about that."

This was the kind of reassurance she sought. She

would survive and grow and live, even if there was no light this morning. But some primal–many would call it superstitious–part of her craved a sign, a symbol that the Gods were on her side.

"You're a very sensitive soul." He was looking slightly above her head, as though he was picking-up something that wasn't discernible with his usual senses. "Do you work with people in some healing capacity?" he asked.

She had never connected the words 'psychology' and 'healing' before. But when she thought about it, it was an apt description. The problem was, that at the moment she was more in need of healing than many of her clients.

"I'm training to be a clinical psychologist. I suppose you could call it a kind of healing."

"Of course it is." He was serious now. "Healing can take many forms. To smile at someone can be healing. To take a child in your arms and rock her to sleep when she's ill is tremendously healing for both mother and child. To give your love and companionship to another human being can be a beautiful, deeply healing experience."

She felt a sharp pain somewhere deep down in her gut. He must have noticed it. He seemed to notice everything.

"It's often a case of 'Physician heal thyself,'" he smiled. "We must all get our own houses in order before we can help another to do likewise. We must recognise when we need healing ourselves."

He said it with kindness. Somehow she felt he knew what she was going through.

"You were talking about love and healing," she said. "Sometimes love can be so painful."

"It's not love but the lack of it that causes pain."

Of course, it was so simple, so true. She could ponder his words for hours. He was speaking again.

"Love is a feeling," he continued. "But there are many forms of love. We can love our parents, our family and our friends. We can love our romantic and sexual partners. It's all chocolates and roses as long as the feelings and the needs are mutual. But this stage rarely lasts. As human beings we have a need to live our individual lives, just as much as we have the need to be part of something bigger than ourselves. When we forget either of these needs we run into trouble. We each have our unique path in life to travel and our unique lessons to learn. But it is equally valid to yearn for union, for oneness. When all needs are sought in the correct place we will be fulfilled. To love another human being with a spiritual intensity and with the expectation that he or she will always take care of you is inappropriate. We are responsible for our own lives."

"As adults, we need to take care of ourselves. If either of us gives away that right or that power to the other, then we are in serious emotional turmoil. When we can find the balance between loving the self and loving others we will no longer experience pain. When we realise fully that we are not alone, that we are part of a divine plan of evolution towards the highest level of light, then we will no longer need to cling to false Gods, in the shape of people, drugs, money, power, or anything else. Then we will be free. We will at last know the truth and only then can we experience true love."

Marion stood there, stunned. She felt high yet balanced, uplifted yet grounded. She had gone to talks on spirituality before and to a couple of meditations. They had been refreshing, full of positive energy and hope. But nothing had matched this degree of enlightenment.

"Everything is put on earth for our enjoyment." He was speaking again. "True love is a gentle, beautiful energy, yet the most powerful feeling of all. Sexual energy is the most urgent and forceful. When accompanied by love it can be both healing and exhilarating. When devoid of love it can be emotionally draining, deadening, even traumatising. Our intention and our level of awareness is everything. We need not deny ourselves anything, though all in moderation. We are free to create either a heaven or a hell on earth. It is our own choice. It is our attitude to life that determines how we see the world. When we know who we really are, Marion, we no longer need to suffer, to form relationships with those who cannot give us love, to work in jobs that do not fulfil us. When we know we are spiritual beings who have chosen an earth existence to further our development, the whole world is set alight for us."

She couldn't help staring at the modern-day shaman, casually dressed in jeans, runners and green woollen jacket. An ordinary man, yet it was his vision that was extraordinarily, revolutionary. She wanted to hear more.

"You've often heard it said that time heals all wounds." He was looking directly into her eyes now. "It's not time that's the healer. It's cleansing yourself emotionally, centring yourself, and integrating your dearly bought experience. I think Kahlil Kibran's quote is beyond comparison: *Your pain is the breaking of the shell that encloses your understanding.* Many of us need pain to motivate us, to bring out the best in us. We're masochists really. But it need not always be that way. Remember: awareness is the key. Then in the course of time we can transfer our romantic energy from the lost love, to a new love, but still retain our love of self."

She nodded. He turned and pointed to the cairn. "Isn't it beautiful? She really shows herself off in the early morning light. The energy is so strong here. It's sparking all over the place. It's a blend of purple and gold." He squinted slightly.

"You can see the colour of energy?" she gasped.

"Yes," he laughed. "It takes a little practice, and trust."

"Purple and gold? How beautiful! They're the Wexford colours," she smiled.

"Is that right?" His eyes sparkled. He seemed to be

enjoying himself.

"How did you become involved in healing?" she asked.

"A lot of factors came together. I had an accident–a car crash. It was a near-death experience. I blanked out. The next thing I remember I was being sucked through a tunnel, with the light growing brighter and drawing me nearer. Then I found myself in another world, a beautiful world. I knew it was my real home. It's the classic tale told by anyone who has passed over for a few moments. I met several beautiful, radiant beings, dressed in golden robes. They told me I couldn't stay there because it wasn't my time. They had other work for me to do."

He smiled again, stroked his beard and continued.

"I was in hospital for about a month. My head was smashed up. The doctors told me how lucky I was to survive. It wasn't luck, I told them. I began reading everything on spirituality I could get my hands on. I had been married for many years but it was going nowhere. We decided to set each other free. Many couples stifle each other's growth. Fear, possessiveness, obsession, boredom, who knows why? Sometimes when you really love a person you realise it's best to let him or her go. When you try and try, and you know in your heart and in your soul you've reached the crossroads, it's a relief to split and to choose a separate path. That takes a lot of courage though."

It was uncanny how he stood there, churning out all these amazing truths. It was as though he could read her mind, or maybe he could see her feelings as a colour? Anything seemed possible now. What would Peter make of all this? Well, she was certain of one thing. Thomas Cleary would give him a run for his money!

"Physical partings can hurt us deeply." His voice was gentle and he radiated a sense of deep calm. "But when we are linked through love there is a part of both people that will always remain connected. That doesn't mean that we cannot live life to the full. The love that is at your core can be shared with another special person, all in good time."

She knew exactly what he meant. She nodded.

"So back to the future!" he laughed. "Then I met a guy who had been to Findhorn in north-east Scotland. It's a healing centre that runs all kinds of courses and it's a way of life for many. It's a beautiful place. So I spent a few blissful months there."

"Isn't that where Mike Scott recorded his album, *Bring 'em all in*? I love his songs," she interjected.

"Yes indeed. I've never met Mike but I've heard lots of good things about him. I love his Waterboys' album, *This is the sea*. He's a regular visitor to Findhorn. It's a very healing place, certainly great for bringing out the creative spirit. There's a lovely stone sanctuary there, set in the midst of nature, where you can place your candle in dedication to the light and meditate. I learned a lot from the people I met there."

"Well, when I returned to Dublin I quit my teaching job and opened a small healing centre. I received insurance money from the accident, so that was adequate until I began making a living from the centre. Now I love what I do. I wouldn't change my lot with anyone. I'll be sixty-five next month. Some of my teaching friends have already retired. They say they feel old, that they're no use anymore, that they're just lounging around waiting for the Grim Reaper to pounce. I tell them to cop on with themselves. Live in the moment! I'm just beginning to live. I've no fear of death because I've no fear of living. I'm too busy to fear anything. And I've too much trust in the sun-God's compassion to worry about anything."

He gave her a boyish wink. She hoped she'd be as bright as Thomas when she was sixty-five: so full of enthusiasm, so alive.

"Brendan said you had some theories on Newgrange." She'd kick herself if she forgot to ask him that.

"Ah yes!" he beamed. "It's not a unique theory. Others have come up with similar explanations. The cairn is carefully constructed over a complex criss-crossing of water flow and energy lines. It's a natural power station for conducting and transmitting energy. It's my theory that the alignment of the standing stones, the quartz facade, the passage and chamber create a huge electrical charge. The effect is greatly magnified when the sun's rays pass through the roof box at the Winter Solstice."

He turned towards the cairn's glinting façade.

"The roof box is made of quartz. Originally many people believe there were two of these quartz blocks. The face of the cairn, as we can see, is built of white quartz, with some parts made of granite. Quartz in its true form is known as rock crystal. X-ray studies have shown that its internal structure grows in the shape of a spiral. Interesting? When crystals are heated, electrical charges are produced. Crystals have been used for millennia for their positive energy. When used in conjunction with human energies they provide a form of natural healing by unblocking the chakras, the human energy field. When light hits the quartz it splits into the colours of the rainbow, glowing and flashing. The outer cairn and the basins of the inner chamber are made of quartz. Basically, Newgrange was built as a conductor of spiralling energy."

Thomas paused, staring at the cairn. He was silent and motionless for a few moments.

"Ah, what energy!" he smiled. "The ring of standing stones around Newgrange acts as a conductor, while the entrance stone is the focal point of the energy. Hence it's spiral facade. Just feel the energy pulsating through this sacred place!"

He closed his eyes. Marion always felt energised and renewed after coming here. Call it energy if you liked. There was something very special about this place, there was no doubt about that.

Thomas was speaking again, continuing to roll out his incredible insights.

"It's the energy that still draws so many here. Some people simply resonate with the same vibration. Imagine what the energy of our ancestors was like? They had waited for days, praying and meditating, raising their God-consciousness, maintaining their pre-solstice vigil, preparing to welcome the source of all life. The energy of the quartz-faced cairn, the sun's first rays of light, the spiritual energy generated by the priests, the priestesses and the healers, and the anticipation of the people that the sun would raise the dead to life must have created an awesome atmosphere".

He paused to look once again towards the cairn.

"When sunlight struck the quartz, a huge blast of energy was transmitted through the cairn. The builders believed that this energy would guide the departing souls on their spiritual journey through the astral plane, to return to the sun. The ultimate symbol of freedom: the soaring of the spirit. I'm sure it was a time when great healing was known to take place. After all, healing requires commitment, dedication and a sacred space. The building of Newgrange fulfils all of these requirements. That same healing energy will be reawakened this morning, as the dawning of another year unfolds. And you, my dear Marion, will be there to taste its sweet nectar."

His words rubbed a cool, silky balm into her chapped soul. His presence was certainly healing.

"Hello again!" It was Brendan.

"Ah! Brendan." Thomas slapped him on the back. "Thanks for introducing me to this lovely lady. We've had quite a discussion since you left."

"It was really great." Marion echoed the sentiment.

"Well, sorry to tear you away, Thomas, but Aisling wants to arrange to see you for healing."

Thomas rubbed his hands together. "It's a busy day so. You're doing a great advertising stunt for me, Brendan. Are you sure you're not making it up so you can have Marion all to yourself again?"

Brendan blushed and didn't answer.

Thomas turned to Marion.

"Enjoy the experience. It's been a real pleasure meeting you. I hope our paths cross again, soon."

"Thanks Thomas, for everything."

She watched as he made his way to the woman who must be Aisling, with the pale golden hair and the long black coat. Brendan remained standing at her side.

CHAPTER 15

Nuala had returned to the gate.

"It's time!" Brendan lowered his voice. "She'll be admitting the privileged few first. Have you got your pass handy?"

"I have it here." Marion's voice was shaky. She was full of nerves. She glanced over her shoulder towards the east. "It's still cloudy. God, I just hope the sun breaks through!"

"Let's send out the good vibes. There's still a chance we'll see it. Now, we'd better get moving."

Nuala was asking those who had passes to step to the front. The media people were all lined up, cameras at the ready. She spotted the cameraman with the beer-belly. He waved to her. She smiled politely.

"There's Murray, the Minister for Hardship!" Brendan pulled at her sleeve. There's always one of them here. "See his State car and waiting chauffeur over there? They've a great time. I should have chosen politics."

She felt a tap on her shoulder. It was Layla, the dark-haired pre-Raphaelite.

"Your big moment has come. Enjoy it!"

Nuala was beckoning for them to go through in single file. Brendan stood back to let her go first. Nuala checked her pass and smiled.

"Straight through, past the visitors enclosure and out through the second gate."

Brendan was beside her again.

"Thomas said there were originally two quartz blocks in the roof-box. Is there any archaeological basis to that theory?" she asked.

"Yes. There's evidence from scratch marks on the surface of the lintel that the quartz blocks had been pulled out and pushed back a few times. That's probably when one of them was dislodged. They also discovered that the corbels behind the roof-box were beautifully decorated. They had never been exposed to the elements so the artwork was in mint condition. They replaced them with replicas. The originals are in the National Museum."

They had gone through the second gate and were now walking uphill, inside the periphery at last.

"It has taken a superhuman effort to restore Newgrange to her former glory," he gestured towards the cairn. "They worked here every summer for four months, from '62 to '75. When they began, the earth was strewn with stones and boulders, the outer cairn had long-since collapsed, and the orthostats in the passageway were reclining inward. It was a long, hard slog to restore her. Some people say she looks too modern. They expect to see a ruin and think in some way that would be more romantic. But, except for the unknown pattern of the interspersed granite rocks on the facade, it's identical to the Newgrange of five-thousand-years ago. Remarkable, isn't it?"

They had just reached the top of the hill. Marion stood back in awe. The cairn's facade glittered, the white quartz glinting in the early morning light. Decorated boulders ran the length of the mound, lying on their sides at the base, about waist high from the ground.

"It's a wondrous creation," she almost whispered.

"The art-work is amazing," he concurred. "So enigmatic. The artists etched their symbols on the kerb stones using blunt tools. Let's walk over to the entrance stone. No matter how many times I see it, I still have to catch my breath. It's probably the finest example of prehistoric art in the world."

They walked to the entrance. The torches still burned there, adding an air of ritualistic expectation. It was a nice touch, though nothing extra was really needed. The cairn itself stole the show every time.

The huge boulder which bestowed the right of passage on all those who were deemed worthy, stood glinting, a proud sentinel in the pale, pre-dawn light. The flowing spirals carved across its surface carried the eye into the centre of the psyche then cast it out again to the far corners of the universe: fluid, graceful, with innate power. Marion wondered, not for the first time, who was the person who lay across the entrance stone, carving with a steady, even hand, creating in smooth, sweeping strokes?

"Magical," she sighed.

"Technology would find that hard to reproduce today." Brendan scratched his head and pondered.

"It's the spirit of the creator that orchestrates its magic. It's more than a symbol on a stone, isn't it, Brendan?"

"It's much more," he smiled. "It's a living monument to the potential of the human spirit. My father often talked about the sad appearance of Newgrange before the excavation and reconstruction took place. It was overgrown with trees and scrub. The tomb exuded an air of decay and abandonment. For me, Newgrange stands as a legacy, not only to the original tomb builders, but also to those who saved her from annihilation. Well, I have to admit I'm biased. The people who led the excavation, like Professor O'Kelly, were my heroes. As a kid, I watched as Newgrange became transformed: an old heap of grass and stones turned into a Mansion for the Gods, right before my eyes. If that isn't magic, what is?"

"I know." She turned to look directly into his eyes. "You love this place. It's in the very fabric of your bones, isn't it?"

"Yes," he nodded slowly. "I see Newgrange as representing all that is noble in human nature. It took the dedication and co-operation of an entire community to build her: men, women and children. Everyone's skills were utilised. Quarrymen and masons located and transported large slabs of quartz from Dublin and Wicklow, and granite from the Mourne Mountains. Structural experts constructed the tomb, placing the corbels, orthostats, roof-slabs, and kerb stones in position. Labourers collected stones and carried them to the cairn, stripped turves and laid them, sealed joints and caulked the roof-slabs. Artists and carvers decorated the slabs, some before they were put in place, others after they had been positioned."

He plunged his gloved-hands into his pockets and looked towards the roof-box.

"The brains or mastermind behind Newgrange", he continued, "the architects and engineers planned every last detail of the project, motivating, leading, and making sure all stages were executed with minute precision. Whether Newgrange was the idea of one person: king, priest, tycoon or political leader, is open to eternal speculation. The sophistication of the workmanship is startling. It required intelligence, a vast range of skills, experience, creativity, ingenuity, and guts."

He paused, then turned directly to Marion. "And belief and love," he added.

She swallowed hard. Here was another kindred spirit. She felt as though she was floating in a hazy dream. This was a strange morning indeed. She yawned, overcome with tiredness and rubbed her eyes. Yet she was still eager to hear more.

"It's all catching up on me, the excitement, I mean."

Her mind was working at two levels. Of course every shred of data she could glean about Newgrange was like gold dust. But there was another side of her that was comparing Brendan to Peter. Intelligence and a love of 'deep' discussion was the point of intersection. There were differences though. Peter had literally oozed charisma. It poured from every sinew. Brendan was much quieter, a few shades paler. It suddenly dawned on her that Peter had been a mass of smouldering emotion, passionate to the core of his being. There were no half measures: either elation or desperation; hot, crackling love or freezing-cold withdrawal. Looking at Brendan, the man in blue who stood pondering the riddles of Newgrange, there was a sense of calmness and stillness about him. What colour was his energy, she wondered? What hidden sides of him would emerge in the crazy oceans of love? Friendship was gentle and safe. Loving with all of your being and opening wide to release the pent-up dam of loneliness: that was the risk and the danger of the unknown.

She took a deep breath and pushed all of her fears to the pad-locked chest at the basement of her mind. He was looking at her again. Perhaps he was comparing her to Terri? Or maybe he too was in need of a friend. We didn't know ourselves, let alone the motivation and driving force behind the person standing next to us, or lying next to us for that matter. All lives were enigmas.

"You're in deep thought," he spoke softly.

"It's this place, where past, present and future meet head-on. I feel I'm in some kind of time-warp."

"It's not the usual Saturday morning experience, is it?" he smiled.

"No. It's the morning when I get my first glimpse of the Holy Grail. And who knows? Life may never be the same again."

"There's a very sad and, if there's even a scintilla of truth in it, quite an ironic theory on what may have befallen the builders of Newgrange." He gazed upwards at the beautifully cut white stones that covered the facade. "We know that only five-hundred-years or so after its construction it was derelict, with Beaker squatters living on the site. Is it possible that the community expended so much energy on its construction that the entire society perished? Crops failed, animals died and their culture was obliterated? There's a similar theory put forward about the demise of the inhabitants of Easter Island. You know those remarkable monolithic stone statues in human form? They were erected in the middle ages, but it's thought that their civilisation crumbled due to their obsession with wonderful works of art..."

Nuala was clapping her hands. She stood on the fourth rung of the row of steps to the left of the cairn. Two rows of wooden steps led upwards at either side of the entrance. After climbing these, another set led downwards, admitting modern-day visitors to the mound. Previously, Marion had read somewhere, the only way to gain entry was to scramble over the entrance stone.

"You are all very welcome to Newgrange on the morning of the Winter Solstice." Nuala's strong, clear voice immediately commanded attention. "At this stage I've met you all, our privileged visitors. We've still about ten minutes to spare before dawn. You can see for yourselves that it's quite cloudy just to the east, so it's not going to be easy for the sun to break through. Anyway, I won't keep you long in the cold but I'll just tell you a little about Newgrange to whet your appetite. Many of you have, I'm sure, heard it all before, so you can just refresh your memories."

"Newgrange is situated on the highest part of this low ridge. The river Boyne meanders across County Meath and on its final stretch it loops south, just after Slane. The land enclosed on three sides by the Boyne contains the passage-grave cemetery, of which Newgrange is the focal point. Knowth, with its seventeen smaller passage-graves, lies one kilometre north-west of Newgrange, and Dowth is to the east."

"Newgrange consists of a passage and a chamber with walls and a roof, and these are built of large slabs.

No mortar was used in their construction. As you can see, a large mound of loose stones covers the tomb. A circle of standing stones surrounds the cairn. The beautiful quartz stones that you see all around you were used to cover the facade and part of the sides of the monument. Elsewhere, ordinary boulders were used."

Nuala brushed a strand of hair from her eyes and pulled her red coat tighter around her. The journalists rested their pens for a brief moment.

"We'll be entering the mound in a moment or so. The passage we'll be travelling through is lined on either side by orthostats. You'd want to place any cameras or bags that you're carrying in front because the passageway is very narrow and we don't want any damage done to the bounders. You'll feel the passage rising upwards when you're walking through. The roof-box, located above the entrance, is so far a unique structure. It puzzled archaeologists for almost one-hundred-years. It's directly aligned with the chamber floor. It is through this slit, in a few minutes time, that the rising sun will hopefully shine and illuminate the chamber."

"Is it looking promising?" The beer-bellied photographer asked.

"We never promise anything. You can see the dark, stubborn clouds hovering to the east, so all we can do is hope they'll clear before dawn."

Marion could feel the butterflies begin to flutter. Tension was rising thick and fast.

"It is most likely that Newgrange was originally built five-thousand-years ago as a mausoleum for a select few, a dynasty of kings perhaps," Nuala continued. "It was probably administered by priests and priestesses. As a monument, it is the coming together of all the spiritual, technical and emotional aspirations of the megalithic culture. It shows a high degree of sophistication in its design, construction, and artwork. Many theories have been put forward as to its purpose and for its artwork's symbolism. Do the three double spirals, which you will see in the chamber, represent the flowing waves of the River Boyne as it loops around the area where the three monuments are situated?"

Nuala glanced at the scribbling journalists. After all her vast experience she knew the kind of poetic snippets to throw them. But there wasn't much time to pause. The race against time was on. Marion spotted Sean Rafter, the guidebook writer, staring up at Nuala. He was hard at work jotting down notes. Yes, there was still a faint look of Peter. But she had done enough reminiscing for one morning. Nuala was speaking again.

"Some say the roof-box was built as a soul-hole to allow the spirits to travel with the sun on this morning. Others say it represents a powerful blend of death rites, cosmic and sexual imagery, and spiritual aspirations to an after-life. Life and death were just two sides of the same coin to the people of Newgrange. The swirling spirals speak of a totality of existence, of life, death and rebirth."

She paused for breath and looked around at the expectant faces gazing up at her.

"I'm sure you all have your own theories about the roof-box, the triple spirals, and indeed the meaning behind the entire monument." Nuala gazed at her rapt audience. "There are a few interesting interpretations of the spirals. They're said to represent a local map of the valley's three tombs, an image of the universe, a symbol of underground water, a diagrammatical symbol of the afterlife and the sign of the triple-Goddess, Brigid..."

Marion nodded at the mention of Brigid. Her old theory had been revealed this day last year to Peter. She tuned back into Nuala's monologue.

"It may denote a symbol of the life-force, without beginning or end, representing infinity and eternal life. All your theories are valid. We'll probably never know for certain the real meaning. It may include a mixture of all of these and more. Okay!"

Nuala pulled back the edge of her red sleeve and glanced at her watch.

"We've about eight minutes to go. So without further ado we'll enter the passage. I'll lead the way. Mind your heads as you're going through. It's very low, especially just inside the entrance. You'll need to crouch down a little."

The experience was reaching crescendo. They began climbing the ten wooden steps, ascending to a small platform and then descending the few stone steps until they reached the entrance.

"After you!" Brendan stood back to let her through.

She crouched down into the passage. It was dark except for a tiny electric light that lit the way. It was rising gently uphill with every step. Quite quickly it narrowed, leaving barely enough room to push through. At either side the pale grey orthostats brushed her clothes and hair. Each time she approached another boulder she feared she'd never be able to squeeze through. She twisted and turned her body. She wondered how the beer-bellied photographer was managing. Was it some illusion, to jog visitors' memories of their initial struggle to push through the birth canal and enter a new world? This is what Peter had believed. Out of the corner of her eye she noticed a few carved decorations on the boulders. No time to stand and admire though.

Suddenly, the passage opened into the brightly lit chamber: the heart of the mound. A swirling sea of stone: yellow, beige, white and grey. She gazed upwards. Within the confines of the chamber, layer upon layer of boulders in the roof created a surprisingly lofty effect. The areas between the boulders were packed with smaller stones, presumably to hold them in place. She peered into the west recess. A delicate pattern of thin circles was carved on the wall. A large stone bowl filled the whole alcove. Some of the boulders beside her were scarred with graffiti, dating back to the seventeen hundreds. She walked towards the back of the chamber and peered inside the north recess. There it was, on the east wall, the famous three-spiralled motif. Jim had bought her a silver brooch replica for her birthday. "It'll bring you luck," he'd promised.

She stood in awe, her eyes winding their way in never-ending loops around the carved whorls. She needed to touch the stone, to make contact with its creator. She slowly traced the spirals with her fingertips. At last, the moment had come.

"It's beautiful." Brendan was beside her again.

"Mm," she muttered. All words had sunk to the bottom of the primordial ocean. Sensation bubbled to the surface, connecting with some ancient, forgotten force.

The chamber was now full to capacity. Cameras were poised at the ready. There must have been about twenty people squashed in. Minister Murray was all smiles, all nods. She could see the headlines now: 'Minister visits tomb of ancient ancestors!' "A good publicity stunt", she thought. "But who wouldn't jump at the chance of setting foot inside the chamber on this morning?"

Nuala still occupied centre stage.

"It was necessary to install an electric lighting system in the passageway and chamber," she stated, "so visitors could inspect the interior of the cairn. As you can see the chamber is cruciform and contains three recesses or side-chambers. Inside the chambers, as well as along the kerb, there are beautiful examples of pre-historic art. There is really nothing uniform about any of the art-works. Originality and uniqueness were certainly attributes that were highly prized by the people of Newgrange."

Nuala's eyes glowed as she spoke. To show this, the eighth wonder of the world, to all who wished to be spellbound by its magic, must have been her special mission in life.

"During excavation the partial remains of at least five

people were found in the chamber." She carried on with her oration, not wishing to leave any stone unturned, on this morning of all mornings. "Who these people were, of course, is pure conjecture: kings, priests, leaders, or people who were honoured for some special ability or quality?"

Marion also pondered who was present in the chamber on this same morning, all those thousands of years ago. Perhaps a spiritual leader or some specially chosen citizen would keep watch, awaiting the dawn to welcome the sun. Surely someone would have been there to witness the miraculous moment?

Nuala was speaking again.

"The sun can shine into the chamber for five days each year, from the nineteenth to the twenty-third of December. For a few days afterwards the sun may be seen in the passageway."

Nuala was inspecting her watch again.

"So far this year the sun hasn't reached the chamber. I must admit I'm pretty doubtful that it will actually happen this morning, but we must try to enjoy the experience no matter what."

Marion could feel her spirits take a sudden dive. She knew the disappointment would be crushing. She'd just have to relish the moment and the honour of being there.

"Now there are just minutes to go." Nuala paused, sizing up her captivated audience. "In a moment I'll turn off the electric light and leave us in darkness. That way you can really savour the atmosphere."

Marion could see the disappointment written all over Nuala's face. She didn't expect it to happen. Her voice shook, just perceptively, and her breathing had become quite shallow. She was tense, expectant, but a little downcast, just like the rest of them.

Marion noticed the beer-bellied photographer standing opposite her. She remembered his odd request to photograph her. She shrugged her shoulders and quickly dismissed him from her mind. Her palms began to perspire, her stomach was all fluttery and her heart was thumping fast. She glanced at Brendan who still stood beside her. He winked and held up his crossed fingers.

"Right!" Nuala smiled. "Are you ready to embrace the moment of truth? Let's prepare to welcome the light."

Nuala pressed the switch. In a moment there was blackness, except for a watery grey line of natural light that crawled along the centre of the sandy floor. An eerie silence took hold, broken only by the sound of breathing, the odd shuffle and ceremonial cough.

As her eyes adjusted to the darkness, visions of faces and places, both unknown and familiar, flashed across her mind: Scenes of vast open fields; thick dense forests; inky-coloured skies full of stars; long fast flowing rivers, so clear that silver fish could be glimpsed darting among the waves; black wolves and red foxes roaming the plains, free and unfettered. And then there was Peter, sipping his pint, smiling, pontificating; his black eyes flashing in soft candlelight. Then she noticed the thick ropes protruding from his body, coming from his genitals, his stomach, his forehead and his heart. Her eyes followed the ropes. She gasped in shock when she realised that they were attached to her own body at the exact same areas. They were still bound together, no matter what the physical distance.

"I can't cut them," Peter was calling to her. "You've got to do it, to set us both free."

From out of the darkness a flaming torch appeared. She took it in her right hand and instinctively held it under the thick strands of rope that joined their genitals. Her hand shook but she daren't draw back. Within seconds the flames had pulled the blackened strands apart. The rope split in two. Next she placed the flame under the rope that protruded from their stomachs. The fire raged and burned for several seconds, finally snapping the charred strands that fell to the floor. The third rope protruded from their foreheads. The flames soared high, singeing the strands, burning, breaking and finally disintegrating.

Now just one rope remained, the one connecting them from the heart. With tears in her eyes she set the flame under the thick, twisted rope. For ages it burned, refusing to break. She looked at Peter. He was crying too. The fire rose higher, consuming, cleansing, setting them free. The strands melted, crackled and finally snapped apart. Peter was standing with arms outstretched.

"I'm sorry, Marion!" he kept repeating.

"It's okay, Peter." She reached out and took his hand, sending him love and forgiveness. She squeezed his hand, smiled up at him, and then let it go. Now there was a path, bathed in pale morning light, roaming through country towns and traversing city streets, mingling with the full spectrum of life. Then the vision faded.

She remembered Brendan beside her. She made a wish that in some way he would be part of her future. She crossed her fingers, closed her eyes and entreated the Gods to send their bolt of light.

A tiny, orange beam, seemingly coming from the floor, greeted her opening eyes. She gasped. Some invisible force was sprinkling a handful of gold dust, transforming the dull gravel into a shimmering mosaic of brilliant light.

"Well, I'll be damned. It's going to be one of those mornings!"

"Christ, we've done it!"

"Wow! Here comes the sun!"

Her fellow pilgrims echoed her sheer delight.

"Oh! you're so fortunate. This is so unexpected," Nuala's voice quivered with emotion. "There's just one thing to remember. Please keep well back from the centre isle because that's the path the sun will travel. We can take turns in moving to the front. Don't worry. We'll have plenty of time. No need to fuss. The whole chamber will be set on fire. This is really quite amazing!"

"You've got your wish, Marion!" A voice spoke through the darkness and a hand reached out to take hers.

"I know, but I can't believe it's happening, Brendan," she whispered, as tears streamed down her cheeks. Their grip became tighter and their bodies instinctively moved closer.

The first slender rays of dawn were slowly unravelling in a perfect symmetrical line across the chamber floor. The thin shaft of light was gradually widening to a beam of dazzling intensity. Cameras clicked on either side. Gasps of amazement, of disbelief, of astonishment and awe filled the chamber. The sun was returning home to awaken the Gods. She recalled the early Celtic legend of *Uaimh na Greine*, the cave of the sun. The rebirth had begun.

Within minutes, the light had spread out, creating a megalithic fan of lustrous colour. Marion stood rooted to the ground, blinking in disbelief. One woman edged her way forward, knelt reverently, and placed a quartz crystal in the centre of the beam. The translucent stone instantly turned to gold, flashing and splintering its tinted light. Marion knelt down too. Brendan did likewise, refusing to let go of her hand. She lowered her head to the floor and gazed along the shaft of light. A carpet of gold assailed her eyes, running the length of the passageway, stemming from an explosion of light bursting through the roof box.

"I still can't believe it," she sighed. "It's so beautiful."

"It had to happen, for both of us." He squeezed her hand and nuzzled closer still.

The rays lengthened and widened, slowly creeping minute by minute until they reached their destination—the central chamber. The entire interior was now completely illuminated in pure, glistening light.

"Glorious!"

"Magnificent!"

"It's like Fort Knox–pure gold!"

"More like the shop window of a jeweller's!"

Aladdin's cave could not have contained such riches. The pale stones of the inner chamber, so accustomed to dwelling in darkness, were now joyously soaking up the light. Each previously white corbel was being magically transformed into amber, citrine, garnet, topaz and ruby. Each glittered and flashed, scattering fire as the light split, creating a prism of coloured brilliance.

Marion glanced at the other spectators of this wondrous event. That awe-struck look was discernible on every face. Each would be touched in some very deep way by the sheer beauty of this experience. Even one of the hardened journalists appeared to have tears in his eyes. She laughed to herself that perhaps for the first time in his career words might possibly fail him, such was the profound effect of this dazzling display.

Everyone present was wrapped, embalmed and bathed in a shower of glistening rays. It was a festival of sparkles–yellow, orange, red, white, cooper, bronze and gold. The entire chamber had suddenly fallen under the spell of the Chief Alchemist. Every corner now shimmered and sparked, reflecting the radiance of their golden master. The swirls, loops and diamonds carved by ancient hands shone in the blaze of the sun, bringing them sharply back to life.

She caught a glimpse of Nuala, standing proudly at the entrance of the chamber, the high priestess presiding over the cosmic feast, personally welcoming the sun on its annual pilgrimage. The light blinded, dazzled and flowed like lasers in long, yellow streaks, piercing the darkness. She turned towards Brendan. He was smiling down at her, his face and hair a rich gold, awash with solar light.

"If this isn't magic!" he grinned. "Look at Murray. Even he is over-come!"

The Minister was tracing the triple spiral with his

fingertips, a look of utter amazement on his yellow-tinted face.

"It's so utterly beautiful," she smiled. "The whole roof is like a giant honeycomb. I've never in all my life seen anything like the colours."

She stood there, arm outstretched, index finger pointing, eyes wide with childlike wonder and hair caressed by solar fire. It was then that Alan Crowley, ace photographer, clicked the button, releasing the shutter. A moment of ecstasy frozen for all the world to see: The sun worshipper.

She could have stood there, soaking in the warm, healing rays of the solstice for all eternity. "If this is the fate of the dead", she thought, "then there is a lot to look forward to." If the kiss of the sun could set the spirits of the dead free, it could surely resurrect her passion and heal her inner wounds.

It lasted but seventeen minutes. Nuala had her predictions down to a fine art. After the pinnacle of the sun covering the entire chamber and infiltrating every crevice of the roof, its descent was gradual but discernible. The light narrowed and reformed into a single beam, slowly receding along the chamber floor and out along the passageway.

The pilgrims crowded around its slow demise. They took it in turns to trace its exit along the passageway. The spirals to the right of the passage had again succumbed to the Midas touch. It took a further ten minutes before the light was finally extinguished. Inevitably, the sun withdrew its splendour and left the cairn again in the hands of darkness.

It was thanks to Nuala's experience that she allowed them to remain for a further few minutes, each one alone in the blackness, absorbing the momentous occurrence. There was ample time to give thanks, to welcome the New Year, to allow the past to fade into its rightful place and the present to be embraced with hope.

The electric light was drab compared to the brilliance that the Father of the Cosmos had bestowed.

"What can I say?" Nuala exalted in another successful solstice. "I'm always so thrilled when it happens. No matter what I say when it fails, the disappointment is enormous. For most, it's a once-in-a-lifetime chance to catch a glimpse of heaven. I know this memory will live with you forever."

Marion felt the tears once again well-up in her eyes and begin to trickle down her cheeks. It had been a tense, emotional morning. It was still only 9.15 but it felt as though she had been waiting outside in the cold, preparing for this initiation for years.

Brendan reached for her hand again and squeezed it.

"What a morning! I feel overcome myself, Marion," he whispered.

Nuala continued her wind-down.

"Well, it's been a fantastic experience and I'm delighted to have shared it with you. After all the years I've been at Newgrange this particular morning always brings an extra rush of blood through my veins and a tear to my eye. For me, Newgrange is always an ancient initiation, a glimpse of divinity."

"A good quote, that," she heard one guy whisper.

Nuala smiled, delighted.

"You can spend a few more minutes inspecting the cairn if you like. I'm sure that some of the people outside are anxious to visit the chamber, even though they've missed the main feature. You can make your own way out within the next ten minutes or so. See you all outside."

She walked towards the chamber opening.

"Happy New Year to you all," she smiled, before being swallowed by the mouth of the passage.

CHAPTER 16

Back through the dimly lit tunnel, crouching, squeezing through; crossing the narrow bridge between two worlds. Back to embrace life, transformed. A blast of light blinded her eyes as she emerged and stumbled up the row of steps. They had been the last to leave the chamber.

Another queue of eager faces had formed at the entrance, awaiting their turn to experience the mysteries of the interior. Brendan's friends were heading the pageant.

"Well Brendan, was it out of this world?" The woman with the golden hair and the long black coat called to him.

"Marvellous, Aisling, the best ever. I'm still in shock."

Nuala was instructing the next relay to move along into the passage. Aisling waved and shouted that they'd call soon to arrange dinner. She gave Marion a quick inspection, smiled, and was gone.

The dawn had left a sparkling morning in its wake: a turquoise sky and white, cotton clouds, complete with shining, yellow sun. From this elevated position the whole surrounding countryside gleamed dark, earthy green, glazed with a melting layer of silver frost. A cold December breeze still tugged and sprayed Marion's hair all over her face.

"Stunning, isn't it?" Brendan stood there staring, transfixed; soaking in the deep emerald balm.

"Incredible!" She breathed deeply, savouring the moment, a wave of calm and peace flowing over her.

"I feel so light, as though I'm floating. I guess I'm high," she laughed.

"Who needs marijuana when you've got Newgrange on the solstice," he smirked.

"Hey there, Marion! How did it go?" Jade, the strawberry blonde, called to her from the kerb. "Nuala said it was magnificent."

"It was even more wonderful than I'd ever dreamt. I'll never forget the colours, the brilliance of the light and the way the corbels in the roof were covered in a glowing sea of gold."

Layla, the dark-haired beauty came up to join them, followed by her entourage of Germans.

"I heard it was quite a performance," she tossed her flowing locks behind her shoulders. "Aren't you the lucky one?"

Marion nodded, giving thanks to the Gods for their generous blessings.

"I'm really thrilled, quite over-awed. It'll take days, weeks and maybe years for it all to sink in. I'm both exhausted and elated."

Christoff, the German guy she'd spoken to earlier that morning, smiled over at her.

"It's great it came true for you. It all worked out, perfectly. That's really good!"

"It's our chance now to bask in the afterglow." Jade began climbing the steps, hoisting up her swirling skirt, her layers of bangles jingle-jangling with every movement. "I'm really dying to see the chamber. Are you lads coming?"

So with Jade self-appointed at the helm, the rest of the crew followed in close pursuit, preparing for entry to another realm.

"Very colourful!" Brendan commented, as Layla's dark head disappeared into the passageway below. "They remind me of some rainbow people I met once. They were travelling all over Europe, awaiting the Age of Aquarius, sleeping under the stars and drinking crystal-clear water from fresh mountain streams. Not a bad way to live."

"Ah! so how was it? Have you been well and truly cleansed with celestial fire?"

Thomas put a hand on Brendan's shoulder. "Or is it all secret, never to be revealed? Daren't you speak of the mysteries that have unfolded on this Solstice?"

"It's the stuff that dreams are made of, Thomas," Brendan smiled. "It's exactly what I needed: a renewal in the power and the generosity of the Gods. Just moments before the sun entered the chamber I had a vision. I saw my parents. They looked much younger than I can ever remember them, as though they'd just stepped out of the photograph that's hanging over the mantelpiece at home. They were in full bloom and bursting with life. They called my name, then each of them hugged me. 'Be happy, son,' my father said. 'We'll always love you. We'll always be there for you. But now you need to plant roots firmly on solid ground. There's a long, brilliant path stretching out before you. Don't be afraid to take it, to live with all your heart.'"

Brendan inhaled the fresh morning air deeply into his lungs and wiped his eyes with the back of his hand. "I never quite expected anything that dramatic," he said.

"Powerful stuff and deeply healing." Thomas patted him on the shoulder again. "I'm delighted for you, Brendan. So it was all worthwhile, getting up at the crack of dawn? Another satisfied solsticer, I'd say!"

"I certainly am." Brendan was smiling again. "I highly recommend it!"

Thomas turned to Marion.

"Was it worth it for you, too?"

"I'm still stunned by it all, Thomas. It was absolutely incredible. I feel I've set a few ghosts free myself this morning. At the very least, I've made a good start."

"Great, Marion."

Thomas now reached across and patted her arm.

"So you both met here this morning to share in this fantastic experience. That's a pretty special beginning!"

He winked at Brendan who blushed and smiled shyly.

"Well, it's my turn to sample the healing energy. Marvellous isn't it?" Thomas walked towards the steps. "If you're not here when I return from my journey to the high-heavens then I'll be seeing you soon, Brendan. And you, too, I hope, Marion."

"He's a lovely guy." Marion waved as he disappeared into the passageway.

"One of the best," Brendan nodded.

"Ah! there you are, Miss." The beer-bellied photographer called as he appeared from the side of the mound. "I'm sure we're onto a winner with that one. A gem if ever I saw it. Can I have your name and address, Miss? I'll send you a copy. No doubt you'll see yourself splashed all over the papers in the morning."

Brendan looked on in amazement.

"So you're a bit of a celebrity?" He raised his eyebrows in mock astonishment.

"Not quite!" She flicked a wavy strand of hair out of her eyes.

Marion gave the photographer her details. She'd love to have a photo of the illuminated interior, just to remember the wonderful colours.

"Yes, I'll send you some extras of the interior if you like," he grinned, seemingly delighted with his morning's work. "Glad to be of service, Miss. Well, I'm heading back to the darkroom now to develop these. Is anyone in need of a lift to Dublin?"

Marion was aware of his eyes darting all over her, making her feel most uncomfortable.

"I was going to phone for a taxi to get back to the